WILD &
CHANCE

WILD & CHANCE

ALLEN ZADOFF

𝔇ɪsɴᴇʏ · HYPERION
Los Angeles   New York

First Edition, April 2020
1 3 5 7 9 10 8 6 4 2
FAC-020093-20073
Printed in the United States of America

This book is set in Sabon LT Pro
Designed by Phil Buchanan

Library of Congress Control Number: 2019955323
ISBN 978-1-368-05319-8
Reinforced binding
Visit www.DisneyBooks.com

For Jeff, Liz, and Sammy

IT'S DARK WHEN I OPEN MY EYES.

Pitch-black, like a night without a moon.

Where am I?

I can't remember anything. Not my name or how I got here. Wherever here is.

I feel a deep, stabbing pain in the base of my skull. It radiates through my head, making it hard to think straight.

Why can't I remember anything?

The floor rocks violently beneath me, causing my stomach to churn.

Get it together, girl!

I steady myself against the swaying motion. That's when the smell hits me.

Diesel fuel. The odor is all around me in the darkness.

Get out!

I start to run, but I jerk to a stop, choked by something around my neck. I claw at it and discover a thick rope tied around me, traveling from my neck to the wall.

1

Who did this to me?

The smell of fuel grows more powerful, and a wave of panic rolls through me.

Calm down. Focus.

First step. Get this rope off my neck. I fight to squirm out of it, and when that doesn't work, I try to undo the knot from the wall.

Not a chance. It's wound tight, rock hard, impossible to unsnarl.

I'm in big trouble.

That's when the idea comes to me.

Teeth.

I can use my teeth on the rope. It's not my favorite idea, but desperate times, right?

I take the rope in my mouth. It's wet with mildew and it tastes like old socks, but the instinct to survive drives me onward. I bite down hard, grinding at the fibers.

My jaw aches, but I don't give up. I chew and chew. The rope softens with each bite, until at last it breaks, and I'm free.

Move!

I run and smash into a wall, slamming my face hard.

Not smart. The headache ratchets up to level ten, but I shake it off and keep moving, feeling my way in the darkness until I find a door. I search for the lever, praying it's unlocked—

The door opens!

I see light ahead. And a staircase.

I race up the steps, away from the sickening diesel smell,

moving toward the light. I pass through an opening at the top of the stairs and pop out into bright sun.

I blink hard, waiting for my vision to adjust.

Details come into focus. Blue sky above, dark water below. I'm on the top deck of a luxury yacht. In the middle of the ocean.

The deck is decorated with expensive furniture, but there's not a person in sight. Who owns a fancy yacht like this, and why is it floating in the middle of the ocean?

I feel like I know the answers, but they're trapped in my head and I can't access them.

That's when I hear it. The sound of a boat propeller fighting through the waves.

I run to the railing just in time to see a speedboat racing away from the yacht. There are four men on the boat—soldiers or officials of some kind. They wear blue uniforms that make them hard to spot against the color of the sea.

"Help! I'm trapped here!"

I shout at the top of my lungs, but the distance and the roar of the engine makes me doubtful they'll be able to hear me.

"HELP ME!!!"

One of the soldiers glances back and elbows his buddy. I see the two of them talking, and a moment later, the speedboat slows and turns, coming around until it faces the yacht.

"Yes! I'm up here!"

I jump up and down, trying to get their attention. For some reason, the boat stays at a distance. One of the soldiers lifts a pair of binoculars and studies the deck of the yacht.

"Please help me!" I race in circles, fighting to be seen behind the railing.

The soldier reaches into a bag and pulls out what looks like a small pistol.

What's he doing?

He lifts the pistol and aims carefully, adjusting his stance several times. Then he fires a red-hot flare into the sky.

At first I think he's signaling to let me know I've been seen, but my excitement turns to horror as I follow the trajectory of the flare. He's aimed too low, and the flare soars through the wind and drifts down toward the yacht, closer and closer, still burning bright.

I smell the fuel around me, and I see the hot light of the flare as it arcs toward the upper deck.

"No!"

There's a loud *whoosh* as the flare hits the yacht and the fuel ignites. The explosion comes less than a second later, a thunderclap that shakes the entire vessel and causes the deck to tilt at a steep angle.

A pair of small boat shoes skid across the deck toward me and catch on a table leg. They are fluorescent-pink children's shoes with hearts painted around the sole.

I have a brief memory of a girl, maybe eight years old with bright red hair, running toward me wearing the pink shoes. She's laughing and holding her arms out to me—

The memory slips away, and I'm back on the burning deck. I look around for the girl, fearful that she might be trapped on the yacht with me. I listen and hear only the cries of seagulls in the distance and the crackling of the ship burning beneath me.

The ship is on fire and it's sinking. I have to get away. But how?

I look over the side at the dark water, angry with white-capped waves. The speedboat with the soldiers is racing away, the vessel no more than a speck on the horizon.

The flare was not a mistake. They were trying to sink the yacht.

I don't understand what's going on, but I know I can't stay here. I peek over the railing and see there's at least a fifty-foot drop to the water below.

Another explosion rocks the ship, and the deck groans in protest.

I have no choice. I have to jump.

Can I survive the fall?

Time to find out.

I back up from the rail, crouch down, and spring forward, muscles rippling in my legs.

The yacht tilts as it takes on water, and I'm suddenly running uphill toward a railing that's rising into the sky. I fight the angle, speeding up and leaping at the last second—

A high-pitched howl comes from deep in my throat as I clear the railing and jump into the unknown.

I LAY PANTING ON THE SHORE.

It's twilight and the wind is blowing along the beach, sending a shiver through me. I'm wet and exhausted from hours on the open ocean, and I need to eat. Or drink. Or both.

Soon.

After the explosion, I paddled away from the sinking yacht and clung to a piece of wreckage, floating with the current, alive but in shock. I held on, kicking, then resting, then kicking again through the night and into the next day. Eventually I saw land in the distance and swam toward it.

Now I'm on this beach, and I'm so thirsty my tongue hangs out of my mouth and touches the sand. An abandoned towel lies next to me. A cartoon blue fish with giant eyes looks up at me, her face half-buried in the sand.

I roll over, using the towel to dry myself off. Then I drag myself to my feet and shake my body, flinging off water in every direction.

I hear voices carried on the wind.

People.

Two kids are throwing a Frisbee down by the water. I get a sudden urge to run down and grab the disk from their hands and play with them. I take a step toward the Frisbee, then I think better of it. It's no time for fun.

Move, girl!

I turn away from the kids and trot across the sand, through a tangle of high grass, and up onto a concrete path that separates the beach from the houses on the other side.

A jogger approaches with a golden Labrador retriever on a leash by his side.

"Excuse me—" I start to say, and the dog explodes in a fit of barking, practically choking himself to get to me.

"What's with you?" I ask him.

The owner pulls the dog back hard, and the two of them run past without speaking to me.

I dart across the path and find myself on a narrow street of dilapidated beach houses. It's getting dark, and I can see families through the windows, moving around kitchens, putting out food, sitting together at tables.

The wind shifts, and I smell meat sizzling on a grill. I follow the scent until I see a family grilling in their tiny backyard. The mother manages the grill while the father puts out plates. There's a dog under the table, a little corgi with a cute haircut. The boy waits until his parents are distracted, then he slips a piece of bread to the dog who hungrily scarfs it down.

My mouth waters as I watch. I get a flash of the redheaded

girl in the pink shoes again. I'm sitting on an expensive marble floor, looking up at her as she smiles at me.

Am I remembering my family?

I draw closer to the boy and his corgi, fascinated. Suddenly the corgi is up on all fours and barking in my direction.

"Shhh," the boy warns her, but the dog ignores him, focused on my scent and barking a nonstop alert.

"Would you keep her quiet?" the boy's mother says.

The boy grabs the corgi's collar and looks around to see what's upsetting her. I silently back up and fade into the night.

I need to figure out why everyone's reacting to me so strangely, but I can't think straight until I get something to eat.

I'm drawn to the scent of garbage cans in the alley behind the house. My mouth waters.

I'm not desperate enough to eat garbage, am I?

I run over to the can, knock off the lid, and dive in.

I guess that answers the question.

My sense of smell is so acute, I can distinguish fresh from rotting garbage inside the bag. I'm disgusted with myself, but it doesn't stop me from tearing open the bag to get at what's inside.

A tiny dog races through the alley toward me, barking at full volume.

"It's just garbage. Don't get excited."

I must be intruding on its territory, because the little thing won't give up.

I turn and roar at the dog, shouting for it to get away

from me. The barking instantly stops, and the dog whimpers and retreats.

"Sorry, buddy."

I notice movement nearby and whip around, ready to defend my smelly treasure. Sure enough, there's another dog next to me, snout-deep in a garbage bag just like me.

"What's up with the dogs in this neighborhood?" I ask. "Why do you guys hate me?"

The dog's mouth moves like it's imitating me.

Strange.

"Are we going to have a problem?" I ask her.

I step away from the can, and the dog steps away.

I shake my head, and the dog does the same.

That's when I realize.

The dog is me.

I'm looking in a broken mirror that's been thrown out in the alley. A long, jagged crack runs down the center of my reflection.

I move closer and examine myself in the cracked glass. I'm a medium-size mixed breed with brown-and-white patches covering a muscular physique. I'm in great physical condition, but I look terrible. I'm dirty and my fur is matted. I lick at myself a little, trying to improve my appearance, but it doesn't help much. Let's face it, I'm a girl in desperate need of a bath.

When I turn my head, I see an ugly wound on the back of my neck, which is probably why I have such a terrible headache. There's also a thick rope leash around my neck with a dangling section that has been gnawed off at the end.

This is the rope I chewed through in the dark earlier.

I stare at myself in the mirror, and I see the familiar brown patches over both eyes and the white stripe that travels down the center of my muzzle. I'm hit by two thoughts at the same time.

1. I'm the same dog, the same girl I've always been.

2. I don't know who that dog is.

I'm horrified to realize I can't remember anything about where I come from or how I got into this situation.

I yelp in pain and frustration, the weird events of the last day catching up to me in a burst of howls. I'm embarrassed to be crying alone in a pile of garbage, but I can't stop.

A loud whistle turns me around. A burly man with a shaved head is coming toward me, and he's smiling like he knows me.

"GOOD DOG," HE SAYS WITH A GRIN.

"Who are you?" I ask, but he doesn't respond.
He just stands there looking at me. Tattoos run the length of both arms, and he wears a sleeveless white T-shirt and long black shorts.

"I think you might be a stray," he says.

Stray. What is that?

"I don't know what's going on," I say. "I think something happened to my head."

He squints at me, curious.

"I need help."

"You're barking a lot, girl. I'm guessing you're hungry."

Barking? I'm talking directly to him.

"Can you understand me?" I ask, slowing down the words in case he's confused.

He looks at me, not comprehending.

This is weird. I can understand everything he's saying, yet for some reason, he doesn't understand me.

The man smells of strange dogs, and I look behind him, expecting to see them. But there are no dogs.

Why would a man smell of dogs with no dogs nearby?

I detect another scent, too.

Fresh meat.

He reaches into his pocket and holds out a chunk of meat in his hand. My stomach rumbles, and my mouth begins to water.

"Do you want something to eat, girl?"

I *really* want something to eat, but who is this guy?

"I help dogs like you," he says as if he can sense what I'm thinking. "Lost dogs. Strays."

"I'm not lost. I just can't remember who I am."

He smiles, again misunderstanding, and he puts the meat on the ground. He backs up a few steps, giving me space.

The man is smiling and his voice is friendly, but I'm suspicious. Why is he in this alley? Why is he talking to me?

But the smell is magnetic!

I edge toward the meat, sniffing. It seems okay to me, so I dart forward and grab the cube. I scarf it down and back up before the man can get near me.

"Wow, you're fast. You've got good instincts, girl."

More meat appears from his pocket. This time he flings it high into the air. I jump for it, all four paws leaving the ground as I snatch it from midair, land, and back away from him in a split second.

He laughs and applauds. "Bravo. My name's Ruben. I've been looking for a dog like you. A dog with game."

"I don't know what game is."

"It looks like you ate right through that thick leash. You must be strong, huh? Strong and agile. I could use a dog like that."

"Use me for what?"

Ruben disappears around the corner without answering, and I follow him, peeking around the wall.

He's standing by a truck with a lightning bolt painted on the hood and an enclosed cargo bed in the rear, the doors open wide. He spills an entire bag of meat cubes across the bed of the truck, and my stomach does somersaults.

"I think you earned yourself a feast," he says. "I'm going to treat you like a *princesa.*"

A wave of dizziness comes over me. My body feels like it's floating, and I'm having trouble concentrating.

Ruben pours water into a bowl, and he gestures inside the truck, offering it to me.

My instinct screams for me to be cautious around him, but it's hard to think clearly with food and water so close—

I give in to temptation and hop into the truck. I bury my nose in the water bowl, tongue lapping at top speed. The bowl becomes two bowls, then three, the images dancing up and down.

"What's happening to me?" I ask. My voice sounds far away, like it's coming from a different dog.

"I've got a good feeling about you," Ruben says. "I think I've hit the jackpot."

I swallow hard, and I notice a bitter flavor in my mouth. There's something wrong with the water, a chemical aftertaste I missed in my desperation to fill my belly.

Get out of the truck!

I panic, knowing I'm in trouble. I try to run, but it's like I'm moving in slow motion. By the time I turn around to jump from the truck, it's too late.

The door slams shut in my face.

I DREAM ABOUT A SOLDIER IN A BLUE UNIFORM.

The dream happens in flashes like a memory that's been chopped into pieces.

At first I see a soldier with blond hair. He's tall and lean in a military uniform, and he calls me by a name I don't recognize.

Next, I am running toward him, breathing hard, anger driving me forward.

A moment later we are on the ground. The blond soldier is beating my chest and screaming in terror.

Why am I attacking this soldier? Why am I so angry?

"Girl!" a man shouts.

The dream disappears, and I open my eyes, my throat still clenched in anger. I don't know where I am, at least until I look up and see the strange man with tattoos looking back at me through the open cargo doors of the truck.

Ruben.

I jump to my feet, ready to attack him for tricking me, but I'm unsteady, and I fall down.

"You were having a bad dream," he says. "You'd better go slow. I put a little something in the food to relax you. It will wear off in a minute."

"You drugged me!" I shout, but the words come out muffled.

I try to open my mouth, but I'm restricted by a leather muzzle over my jaw. I shake my head, trying to get it off me.

"I put some gear on you. It's a safety issue until we get to know each other better."

Know each other? Why would I want to know you?

"I got rid of that ugly wet rope you were wearing, too. Put a black leather collar on you to give you an edge. Ruben takes care of his animals."

I get to my feet slowly, the dizziness lessening.

The moment my vision settles, I make a break for it, trying to dart past him. He yanks an unseen leash and pulls me up short, surprising me. The leash is attached to my new collar. I choke and growl, fighting him.

"You're angry. That's good. You'll need that anger in a few minutes."

What's happening in a few minutes?

He pulls at the leash, forcing me to jump from the truck.

We're in a large dirt lot with fancy cars parked in neat rows. The air is filled with the smell of expensive leather as we weave between BMWs, Teslas, and Porsches. For some reason I recognize cars like these. Some part of me wants to hop into the backseat of the Tesla and settle down for a ride.

Have I been in a car like this before? I try to remember, but nothing comes to me.

We approach a large warehouse and a thick man in a three-piece suit steps out and blocks the door, a bulge under his shoulder.

It's a gun.

I pull back on the leash, recognizing the weapon and the danger it poses.

"You know he's packing, huh? I hope you're not a police dog," Ruben says under his breath.

The man greets Ruben with a wave, and I growl at him.

"Easy, girl," Ruben says.

The man at the door just laughs. "She got something against a good-looking man in a suit?"

"Maybe it's the cologne, Vasily. I could smell you across the parking lot."

"I want to smell good for our fancy clientele."

"You can smell like them, but you'll never be one of them."

"Ain't that the truth. For both of us."

Ruben grunts and adjusts his belt. "Full house tonight?"

"Full house and deep pockets. Didn't expect to see your face around here again. I heard you gave up the wrestling game."

Ruben shrugs. "I owe some people, you know?"

"The kind of people who play rough. Watch yourself, my friend."

"I hear you. But I've found a special dog this time. Wait until you see what she can do. One last match, then I'm gone like the wind."

Vasily looks me over and sighs. "I hope she can get you out of trouble."

"Me, too," Ruben says, and Vasily swings open the steel door.

We step through the entrance into chaos. The air is filled with the scent of dogs. They are everywhere inside, big dogs wearing muzzles, restrained by rough-looking men and women who hold them on short leashes. I recognize breeds like pit bulls, rottweilers, and Dobermans. I can feel their excitement at being here. They pivot this way and that, snapping at one another when they cross paths.

There's a raised platform on one end of the warehouse where a tuxedoed bartender pours cocktails for a group of people in expensive clothes. The crowd mills around, chatting and drinking as they look down at the noise and chaos below them.

I'm instantly distrustful of these wealthy people. What are they doing in a warehouse filled with dogs?

A woman in a sleeveless vest blocks Ruben's way, a gray rottweiler by her side. The huge rottie sports a thick chain collar and a muzzle with silver spikes. He's nearly twice my size, and he stares at me over the muzzle with undisguised hatred.

"What's with you?" I ask him, but he doesn't respond.

"I thought they ran you out of town," the woman says to Ruben.

"I don't run, Jackie. Not when I have this kind of talent. Meet La Secreta."

Jackie reaches toward me, and I jerk away, not wanting to be touched.

"She's nervous for a wrestling dog. Maybe the secret is she's part Chihuahua."

"She's special. You'll see."

Jackie scoffs and walks away.

"I hope I'm right about you," Ruben says.

A loud whistle cuts through the noise. A heavy man in a tuxedo shouts, "Take your places, ladies and gentlemen!" The wealthy crowd cheers and rushes down the stairs from the platform, fanning out around the warehouse.

"That's the Commissioner," Ruben says. "We have to get ready."

"Ready for what exactly?" I ask.

He pulls me through the crowd, and I have no choice but to follow, still dizzy from the drugs and not yet fully in control of my body.

Ruben stops briefly to slip money into the Commissioner's pocket. The two of them exchange a wink and a nod.

"Change of roster," the Commissioner shouts. "First match will be Thunder versus Secreta!"

"Match?" I say.

The room erupts with shouts as money is waved in the air. I hear a hundred simultaneous conversations, people discussing the merits of my physique versus Thunder's and predicting how long it will take Thunder to win.

Thunder and Jackie position themselves on one side of a dirt pit, while Ruben takes us to the other. Jackie pulls a leather vest on Thunder. There are storm clouds painted on its sides.

"You gotta be kidding me," I say.

Ruben leans down and whispers in my ear. "I owe a lot of money, girl. They would have broken my legs if I didn't bring a dog tonight."

"I'm sorry you're in trouble, but what does it have to do with me?"

"I know you can't understand any of this," he says, "but you're getting me and my family out of a jam. I just need you to stay in the match for two minutes. It's like wrestling, only with dogs. Keep your head down and do your best."

I look into his eyes and see the sincerity there, but whatever is going on with this man and his family, I can't forgive him for putting me in this situation.

"Release!" the Commissioner screams, clapping his hands together.

Ruben unsnaps the muzzle and whips off my collar in one motion. He aims me toward the center of the ring.

"Get him, Secreta!"

"Not a chance," I say, and I go in the opposite direction, looking for a way out.

The crowd yells at me and surrounds the pit, packed in tight. There's no way to get past them.

I hear a roar and I spin around. Thunder is racing toward me at full speed, his vest flapping around at his sides. He's so fast he covers the distance in a few seconds.

"Stay back," I warn him, but he can't understand me. I bark instead, a deep staccato warning that he ignores.

He's nearly on top of me, and I react without thinking. I pivot left, avoiding the head-on attack. Thunder is moving too fast to stop and he runs past, crashing into the dirt where I was standing a moment ago.

I hear laughter in the crowd, punctuated by the enraged snorts of Thunder.

It's been less than fifteen seconds, and Ruben said I had to last for two minutes. Maybe I'll be able to dodge Thunder for another minute—

"Watch out!" Ruben shouts, interrupting my train of thought.

I whirl around to see Thunder coming at me again, chest heaving.

For a split second, I don't know what to do. Then something inside me shifts, and I feel rage in the back of my throat.

Fight! My instinct demands, and I imagine myself taking on this dog, knocking him back or maybe even taking a bite out of him—

What? No!

I'm not going to fight a dog I don't even know. I dart to my right, hoping to avoid Thunder again. But the big rottweiler learned from his last attack, and he pulls up short, stopping his charge and bringing us face-to-face.

He's smarter than I thought. I cut left and right, and Thunder does the same, matching me move for move, edging me back against the circle of screaming bystanders. I try to run between their legs to get away, but they kick at me, boots connecting with my hindquarters.

I hear snorting behind me, and I have no choice but to turn and face Thunder.

The rottie is three feet away in a low crouch. The moment

I turn, he leaps at me, mouth open wide as he springs for my neck.

I hesitate for a moment, shocked by the violence I see in Thunder's face. This is no wrestling match for him. It's more like life or death.

I feel a hot energy surge through my body. It seems there's no way to escape this fight, but I no longer want to escape.

I want this dog's throat in my teeth.

Attack!

This time I listen to my instinct, and I push off my front paws, meeting Thunder's leap with my own. My smaller size and greater agility allow me to come up from below and surprise Thunder as my teeth close around his throat. He whimpers beneath my bite, afraid for the first time.

My stomach churns, sickened by the anger I feel. Thunder squirms in my grip, snarling as he fights to get free. I can hear the shouts of the crowd demanding that I finish him off. All I have to do is bite down—

No!!!

I twist to the side, flinging Thunder away from me, hearing him yelp as the big dog goes airborne across the pit, landing hard and spinning through the dirt. He crashes into Jackie, and the two of them go down in a heap.

The crowd gasps and falls silent.

What just happened?

I look back at Ruben. He's as surprised as I am, watching me wide-eyed.

"Did you see that?" he says, elbowing the man next to him. "She just tossed a giant dog like it was nothing.

I knew she was something special the first time I saw her!"

I can still taste Thunder's fur in my mouth. Memories of past fights flood my mind, but they are as vague as shadows.

Have I killed before?

The idea repulses me, and I shake the thought away, whipping my head from side to side. I cough and drool, trying to clear the taste of strange dog from my tongue.

I turn and walk back toward Ruben, relieved that the match is over, but a handful of people in the crowd are pointing across the pit at something behind me.

Jackie is splashing cold water on Thunder, reviving him. He jumps back to his feet, and she urges him into the ring to continue the fight. A ripple of delight passes through the crowd.

Thunder rushes at me, his paws slamming the dirt as he accelerates to full speed.

We're only a minute into the match, but I can see it's not going to end well. Thunder won't stop unless I stop him.

Permanently.

I scan the room, looking for other options.

A flash of light from above catches my eye. There's a window high on the warehouse wall, covered in chicken wire. A streetlight shines through from the other side.

A plan comes together.

I let Thunder get close, waiting until the very last second, and then I jump up. I step on Thunder, using his back as a springboard, and leap at the Commissioner, who is watching from just outside the pit.

The man screams and ducks his head to protect himself,

and I push off his shoulder, using the momentum to go even higher, jumping from his shoulder to a ladder rung, to the top of a stack of boxes. I spring up at the window, afraid the chicken wire is going to catch me and knock me back to the ground.

I pull in my front paws and hit the wire with my chest, feeling the sharp metal and glass scrape my skin as I crash through both layers and sail into the night air.

I'm out! I made it!

I come down hard on the roof of a Mercedes SUV, the metal crunching beneath me and absorbing my impact.

That's gonna leave a mark.

I leap to the ground and keep going, racing through the parking lot and onto a nearby street, not stopping until the shouts from inside the warehouse fade behind me, replaced by the sound of my heart beating as I run free into the night.

I GET AWAY FROM THE WAREHOUSE.

My body aches from the fight and from the impact of crashing through the window. When I'm far enough to be safe, I curl up and lick myself, assessing the damage.

I'm scratched up pretty good, but the wounds are superficial.

I'm shocked by the rage I felt in the ring, and also by my incredible physical skills. How was I able to take on a rottweiler that was nearly twice my size?

Even stranger, why can I understand people when they can't understand me?

I search for answers inside myself, but my memory is as foggy as it was when I first woke up on the yacht.

I hear a boy's voice shout from somewhere nearby.

"Give it back to me!"

My ears perk up with curiosity. I take a step toward the shouting, but I stop myself. I can't trust people after what I've just been through, and I want to avoid any problems.

"Help!" the boy shouts, his voice high-pitched and afraid.

I shiver and my fur stands up.

It's a child. In trouble.

I pause in midstride, instinct pulling me toward the voice rather than away. I turn the corner to have a look.

Three older kids confront a skinny young boy who is backed up against a wall.

One of the kids has something that the boy wants. It's a silver cell phone that glints in the streetlight.

The older kid holds it up, high out of the boy's reach.

"I need it back!" the skinny boy says.

"I *neeeeed* it," the older kid says, mocking him.

"I'm waiting for a call!"

The older kid puts the phone to his ear, pretending to receive a call. "Hello, Puberty? I'm scared, could you come back in a few years?"

"You're gonna break it!" the skinny boy screams, and he grabs for the phone, unintentionally bumping into the older kid.

Without warning, the older kid punches him in the stomach, doubling him over. The boy tries to get away, but he's trapped between a brick wall and the three kids hovering over him.

"This is not your business," I say to myself, but something won't let me leave.

A low growl rolls from my chest, and the gang of kids turn toward me.

"Leave him alone," I warn them.

"Stop barking at me, mutt," the older kid says, and he

punches the boy in the side. The boy gasps for air and drops to the ground, hitting his face on the pavement.

Something snaps inside me, and I'm overwhelmed by a desire to protect the skinny boy against his stronger opponents.

I dart between the attackers' legs and stand next to the sobbing boy on the ground.

The three older boys look at me, startled.

"Is this your attack dog or something?" they ask him.

The boy squints, surprised to find me next to him. His brown hair falls across the bruise that's forming near his eye. He blinks, uncertain of where I came from.

I edge closer, silently communicating that I'm here to help.

"Yeah, she's my dog," he says, picking up on my energy.

"Bullcrap," the oldest kid says. He shouts and stamps his foot to shoo me away.

"Nice try, kid," I say, and I bare my teeth and roar at full volume.

He goes pale, and he drops the silver cell phone and backs up. His friends do the same.

"To heck with it," the older kid says. "I'm not in the mood for rabies this week. Let's go, guys."

"We'll kick your butt later, Chance," one of the other kids says.

Chance? Is that the boy's name?

The kids walk away, and my rage dissolves. Chance whimpers on the ground next to me. Before I know it, I'm whining along with him.

He looks at me strangely. "Why are you crying?"

"I'm not sure."

It's some kind of instinctual bond, and I can't help it.

Chance sniffles and stops crying, and I do the same.

"Weird," he says, then he pulls himself to all fours and looks around.

I can hear the older boys' footsteps moving away down the street.

"Why did you help me?" he asks.

"Maybe I don't like bullies," I say.

He looks at me strangely. "You bark like you're trying to talk to me. Or maybe I just got punched in the head and I'm imagining things."

He checks the street around us, then he groans and gets to his feet. He immediately grabs for the cell phone, snatching it from the ground and bringing it up to his face, frantically pressing buttons.

"Come on, come on," he says, biting his lip. It takes a moment before the phone comes on, bathing his face in a blue glow.

"Yes! It still works."

I watch him, intrigued by his energy, intense yet vulnerable.

"I keep my phone on all the time, even when I'm sleeping. Just in case my mom needs someone to talk to."

He wipes the screen on his shirt and, satisfied that it's working, puts it safely away in his pocket.

"I should call the cops on those guys, but I can't risk getting in trouble," he says, and then he laughs. "Nice move, Chance. First you get beat up, and now you're talking to a dog. You have definitely lost your mind."

He rubs dirt from his hands, shakes the gravel out of his hair, then he turns to leave.

I whimper at the thought of being alone again. The sound embarrasses me, but I can't stop.

Chance pauses. "Whoa, what's going on with you?"

"I don't know," I say. I turn away from him and bury my face in my front paws, ashamed to be seen crying.

"I'm sorry, girl. I wish I had some way to say thanks, but I don't have any food, and I can't—"

He kneels in front of me, his voice low.

"Are you a stray?"

Stray. There's that word again.

He studies me in the light of the streetlamp.

"It looks like you were in a fight like me. Are you hurt?"

He reaches for me, and I growl, warning him back. Despite how much I'm hurting, I don't want to be touched by a human. Not yet at least.

"Easy there," he says, pulling his hand back. "My name's Chance."

"I don't know my name."

"No collar, no tags. I don't even know what to call you," he says.

I look down, disappointed.

"Too bad we can't talk to each other," Chance says.

I whimper out of frustration. Chance reaches out to comfort me, but I jerk back again.

"You don't like to be touched, do you?"

My reactions are confusing me. I want to be touched, but I don't trust anyone.

"I get it," Chance says. "It's tough when you don't have a home. And it's probably scary out on the streets, right?"

He stands, and something on the back of my neck gets his attention. "You have this thing—it looks like a burn mark—on the back of your neck."

"That's why my head's been killing me," I say.

Chance frowns in disgust. "Who would do this to a dog?"

It's a good question. *Who did this to me, and how can I find them?*

"I have to get home," Chance says. "I wish I could help you, but my situation is messed up. If I get in trouble—Anyway, it's complicated."

He stands, hands on his hips as he looks down at me.

"Tell you what. I'll come back tomorrow with some food. If you're still around."

"I'd like that," I say, but even as the words come out of my mouth, I realize it's not going to happen. There's no way I'm going to stay in the area with Ruben and the warehouse people nearby. I don't know where I'm going next, but I know I'm not staying here.

"Okay, then," Chance says. He takes a step, then hesitates, talking to himself. "Don't be stupid, Chance. You're not allowed to have any pets."

He turns and starts to walk away.

A high-pitched engine noise echoes off the alley walls around us. We both look up at the same time as a mysterious blue van glides slowly across the entrance to the alley, its windows blacked out.

Something about this van is familiar. The fur on my back

stands up, warning me of danger. Instinctively I move deeper into the shadows.

"Do you know them?" Chance whispers. He follows my lead, pushing himself up against the wall next to me.

"I have a bad feeling," I say.

The back doors of the van come into view. The words *Animal Control* are painted in white letters across the rear.

"What's Animal Control doing out on a Saturday night?" Chance asks.

A spotlight snaps on from the top of the van, and a bright white beam shoots down the alley, scanning from side to side.

"Run!" Chance shouts.

"You don't have to tell me twice."

I sprint down the street with Chance right behind me, the two of us staying just ahead of the spotlight as we race out the back of the alley.

We hit the main street and keep running, side by side, until we've crossed several intersections and we're sure the Animal Control van isn't following us.

IT'S GETTING LATE.

I walk with Chance for a while, judging it safer to have a person next to me than to be alone on the streets at night.

I need to find a safe place to bed down. Maybe with a good night's sleep, I'll remember enough to be able to plan my next move tomorrow.

The neighborhood changes from warehouses and stores to small homes. We walk down a street of dilapidated houses packed together with barely any space between them.

In the window of one of the houses, a little girl is jumping up and down on a bed, waving her arms, while her mother pleads with her to stop. I watch the silent pantomime, the mother's mouth moving, the girl singing, the mother's frustration turning to laughter as she joins her daughter in song.

"You miss your home, don't you?" Chance asks.

His voice startles me, and I look away from the window, confused. How can I miss a home I don't even remember?

"I guess dogs have feelings, too," Chance says. He bites his lip, thinking hard. "Maybe I can sneak you into my house for one night. We can look for your real home tomorrow before that Animal Control van finds you."

I like that Chance doesn't treat me like I'm stupid, even though he has no way of knowing how smart I am.

"Do you want to come home with me?" Chance asks. "Not forever, but just for now?"

Just for now.

My instinct warned me not to trust people. I didn't listen earlier, and I ended up with Ruben. But as I look at Chance biting nervously at his lower lip, my instinct tells me something different.

Trust him, it says.

I wag my tail to let Chance know I'm willing. Just for now.

"I guess that's a yes," he says with a laugh. "If we're going to be hanging out, I think I need to name you."

"Name me?"

"I'll call you Wild. That's how you looked when you scared those dudes away. Like a wild animal. But you're not really wild, are you? You're a good dog."

I don't know what kind of dog I am, but I can't remember my own name. Besides, Wild sounds kind of cool.

"Wild. It'll be our little joke."

I yip quietly to let Chance know I approve.

He smiles and reaches out to pet me, but I pull back, staying just out of reach.

"I get it," Chance says. "No more touching. I promise."

CHANCE LEADS ME THROUGH THE SHADOWS ON THE SIDE OF A HOUSE.

This house is bigger than the ones around it, but similarly run-down, surrounded by a yard that's unkempt and overgrown with weeds. We walk between rows of bushes until we come around to the back door.

"Why are you sneaking into your own house?" I ask.

He shushes me with a finger to his lips. Then he quietly opens the door and motions for me to follow him inside. We run through a musty living room full of old, worn-out furniture, then we scurry past a room where a few boys lounge, and scamper upstairs.

Chance opens the door to a bedroom, guides me inside, then quickly closes it behind us.

"This is my room," he says.

I look around the small bedroom, trying to find out more about him, but there's nothing personal in here. There are no posters, no books, no photos, not even a tablet to watch movies on.

"It's called a group home. I'm only here for a little longer."

"A group home? I've never heard of that."

Instinct takes over, and I sniff my way around the small bedroom, inhaling the scent of desperate children who have lived here before. I see their faces like faded pictures, their expressions angry, afraid, lost. I whimper, overwhelmed by the emotion lingering in this place.

"What's wrong, Wild?"

Chance looks at me with concern. I shake my head, flopping my ears and jowls to disperse the scent.

"You probably smell a lot of different people. Kids move in and out of this place all the time. I'm looking forward to the 'out' part of the equation. I'm going to see my mom on Thursday. That's why I have to play by the rules."

He opens the closet door. "I think we should put you in here," he says. "Just in case someone comes in."

I back away, thinking about being locked in Ruben's truck earlier. I won't allow myself to be trapped again.

"There's nothing to be scared of," Chance says. "It's just an old closet."

Chance walks inside and turns on a light. He picks up a bunch of dirty clothes to clear some space.

"I've never had a dog before, but I think dogs like to sleep on something soft, right?"

He takes a blanket off the shelf and lays it on the floor for me to use as a bed.

I stand outside the closet, watching him arrange it for me.

He can sense my hesitation, so he steps out and moves away, inviting me to check it out.

I stare at the entrance, reluctant to go inside.

"I get it," he says. "I have an idea."

He takes a wooden hanger and puts it on the floor where the closet door meets the wall. Then he shows me how it won't click shut with the hanger in the way.

"This way you won't get locked in."

I edge forward, sniffing my way into the closet.

"I'm sorry you have to stay in here, but if my house-mother—"

There's a hard knock at the door, and Chance jumps to shut the closet door, leaving a small gap.

"Please don't make any noise, Wild."

A second later, I hear the bedroom door open.

"Lights out," a woman says sternly.

I sense her energy fill the room, angry and unstable, and it makes me agitated. I press my eye to the crack and watch her. She has a face like a bulldog, and a big black hairdo that resembles an army helmet.

"Yes, ma'am," Chance says.

The woman surveys the room, suspicious. "What kind of trouble are you getting into up here?"

"No trouble."

"What happened to your eye?"

Chance quickly covers his face, trying to hide the black-and-blue mark where he was punched earlier.

"I guess I fell," he says.

"Again?" the woman asks. "What will social services say if I return you with bruises all over your body?"

I want to bark at her to make her shut up, but I don't want to get Chance in trouble.

"You're out of here in five days," the woman says. "Try not to walk into any more walls."

She goes out and closes the door behind her.

I push open the closet, and Chance frowns.

"That's the housemother," he whispers. "I call her the Wicked Witch of West LA."

He walks to the bedroom door. "I'll get something to clean you up. Back in a minute."

Chance goes out and leaves me alone in his bedroom.

I sniff at the blanket on the closet floor. It smells like the room, a combination of sweat and fear from the children who have lived here.

I don't like the smell, so I sniff my way across the room, following Chance's scent to his bed. I hop up where the scent is stronger. Chance's smell is comforting to me, and I move around on the mattress and feel it bounce beneath me. I jump up and down a few times, enjoying the feeling of going airborne with little effort.

I land on Chance's pillow, and the softness sends a ripple of pleasure through me. The exhaustion of the day pulls at me, and I yawn and stretch.

I probably shouldn't do this, but I take Chance's pillow between my teeth, hop down from the bed, and carry it into the closet with me.

I settle down on the pillow with my head between my front paws. I try to stay awake until Chance gets back, but I can't. Before I know it, I've fallen asleep.

I DREAM OF THE BLOND SOLDIER.

He wears a blue military uniform and calls to me from across the room. It's the same dream I had earlier, only with more detail this time. The soldier makes hand signals as if he's giving me commands. When he turns, I see the initials AC on the sleeve of his uniform, and I'm overcome with an intense feeling.

Hatred.

I run toward him, and he shouts for me to stop, but I speed up and attack, diving for his midsection, jaws snapping.

"Wake up, Wild!"

I open my eyes to find a boy I don't recognize facing me. I'm still in the dream, teeth bared, growling.

"It's Chance! Remember?"

The boy seems to know me, but I don't remember him. I see a human being, and the dream has me wanting to hurt humans, make them feel pain like I've felt. I open my mouth to attack—

"Stop!"

I freeze with my jaws open, wanting to bite but fighting the impulse as my brain catches up to my body.

I blink and shake my head. The boy's face slowly comes into focus.

"Chance, I'm sorry."

He's standing in the closet door, shaking with fear.

"Did I hurt you?" I ask.

The look on his face says it all. He's not hurt; he's terrified.

I yelp and put my head between my front paws, pressing my face to the ground in apology. I almost hurt this boy who's done nothing but help me.

"You're back," he says, obviously relieved. "You didn't seem like yourself for a second, Wild. You were like a whole different dog."

I'm afraid he might be right. There's a different dog inside me. A dog who rages and knows the taste of blood.

A bad dog.

"It was probably just a nightmare," Chance says.

I'm not so sure. I've had memories of the blond soldier a few times now. None of them good.

"I have bad dreams, too," Chance says. "They're scary, but they're not real."

I want to believe him, but I'm not convinced.

He opens the door wide, inviting me to stretch my legs. He looks behind me to the floor.

"Hey, you stole my pillow."

I lower my head and whimper.

"No big deal," he says. "You can borrow it until we get a bed for you."

He sits on the edge of the mattress and unplugs his cell phone from its charger. He stares at the screen.

"Like I said, I keep it on in case my mom needs to talk. We have a scheduled call every Sunday, but I worry about her, you know?"

I feel really bad for Chance. I can see he's doing his best to deal with a difficult situation.

"She isn't a bad person, Wild. She's an addict. The drugs make you do things you wouldn't do if you were thinking straight. That's what she told me."

I come forward to smell him better.

"She's been clean for ninety days, so now we can have a hearing and the court might let us live together again."

Chance slides down to the floor at the foot of the bed. He points to the room around us.

"This place sucks, Wild. I have to get out of here."

He puts the phone back on the dresser.

"I wish you could understand me," he says.

"I wish you could understand me, too."

He yawns and climbs into bed.

"At least you're a good listener," he says with a laugh. "Maybe all dogs are. I don't know exactly, because I've never had one before."

He yawns again, then he rolls over and turns off the lamp. The room is lit by the glow of his cell phone.

"We're going to find your home tomorrow. I have an idea where to start."

His voice trails off, replaced by the sound of snoring.

A part of me wants to get closer to him. It's a different kind of instinct, a softer one. For some reason, I don't trust that feeling.

For now, it's better to stay away, to protect myself.

After the nightmare I had, maybe I need to protect Chance, too.

I retreat into the closet and turn a couple of times to spread my scent before I'm ready to settle down.

I fall asleep, listening to Chance breathing, hoping the blond soldier does not visit me again in my dreams.

CHANCE TAKES ME TO DOWNTOWN SANTA MONICA.

We walk the streets together, watching as people rush to work and cars honk as they fight through traffic.

"I figured we'd walk around a little, and maybe you'd recognize something," Chance says. "It might help lead us to your home."

I sniff my way down the sidewalk, following the scent of neighborhood dogs. The scent grows stronger as I move forward.

"Hey, where are you going?" Chance asks, but I don't stop, racing past him and turning the corner onto a busy street. The dog scents merge together into a busy canine highway, and I hurry on, excited to follow the trail.

"Slow down, Wild! I only have two legs!"

The scents burst to life, I turn into a large parking lot filled with cars, and stop.

"What do you—" Chance stops next to me.

We're standing in front of a bright white store that runs the length of the block. A sign reads PETSTAR SM. Images of dogs, cats, birds, and fish appear on screens across the front of the store, one shifting into another in a digital montage.

"You found a pet store," Chance says, surprised. "Have you been here before?"

I'm seized by déjà vu as I look at the store. It feels like I know this place, but I can't be sure.

I watch as animals of all kinds enter the store, each of them accompanied by a human who cares about it. I whimper and sniff the air, wondering if there's a person who cared about me. If I find that person, I'll find out who I am.

The thought gets my heart racing excitedly, and I trot toward the front entrance of the store.

"Geez, wait up!" Chance says.

The door slides open, and I'm hit by a wave of ice-cold air-conditioning.

"She needs to be on a leash," the guard says, stepping in front of me.

"Um, that's why we're here," Chance says. "I'm buying her one."

"New dog?" the guard asks.

"Second day together," Chance says.

"A rescue, I hope?"

"Yep, she rescued me," Chance says.

The guard grins and motions us through. "I'll make an exception just this once. Leashes in aisle seventeen."

We walk into a massive store with pet products as far as the eye can see.

"This place is ridiculous," Chance says.

There's a bright green stuffed turtle on a shelf in front of me, and I dart forward, grabbing it and giving it a playful squeeze.

"What are you doing?" Chance asks.

"I don't know," I say through gritted teeth.

I snap my head back and forth, feeling the foam in the turtle squishing between my jaws.

"We haven't paid for that," he says, and he pulls it away from me and puts it back on the shelf.

"Sorry," I say. "It just felt really good."

I hear footsteps behind us, and I turn to find a smiling young employee. His face is dotted with acne, and he smells like orange soda and pepperoni sticks.

I don't care much for the orange soda, but the pepperoni sticks smell delicious.

"Welcome to PetStar, where your pet is the star of the show," he says. "My name's Myron."

He looks down at me, and his energy changes. He seems nervous as he stares at me.

"Do I know you?" he asks.

I look at his name tag.

Myron, Groomer

It doesn't ring any bells for me.

"I don't think so," I say.

"She's brand-new," Chance says, covering for me.

Myron glances at me again. His breathing quickens, and he nervously taps his foot on the ground.

What's wrong with this guy?

Myron gulps and pulls himself together. "If this is your first time, you're entitled to a free grooming."

"We don't need a grooming," Chance says.

"Sure looks like she could use one."

I snort, offended by his comment. Then I look down at my coat and see my fur is matted and dirty. I shake myself and dust particles fly into the air.

Maybe I could use a little shampoo after all.

"You happen to be talking to Magic Myron, the fastest groomer in the store. I'll wash her and have her back to you in no time."

I look up at Myron, and he winks at me.

Okay. Weird.

"She doesn't like to be touched," Chance says.

"We see that all the time," Myron says. "It's not a problem. Give me twenty minutes, then you can pick her up at Mar del Mutt."

He points to a small pen of dogs running back and forth in a fake beach scene complete with a plastic palm tree.

Chance looks nervous. "Is that okay with you, Wild?"

Something is definitely going on with this Myron guy, and I want to know what it is.

I wag my tail to signal Chance.

Myron smiles. "Looks like she's fine with it."

"I guess," Chance says.

"Her name's Wild?"

Chance nods.

"Wild and I will see you soon!" Myron says.

Chance heads down the aisle, looking back twice to make sure I'm okay.

The moment he's out of earshot, Myron leans down.

"Is it really you, Honey?"

Honey?

He looks at me like he recognizes me. I feel excitement bursting in my chest. "Do you know me?"

"You missed your last grooming, and I thought you were—"

Sweat breaks out on Myron's forehead, and he doesn't finish the sentence.

"You thought I was *what*?" I say, anxious to hear what he knows, but I can tell from his expression that he can't understand me. Just like everyone else.

"We shouldn't be out here where they can see us."

He motions for me to hurry, and then he heads down the aisle, disappearing behind a door marked THE GROOMING GROTTO.

Does Myron know who I am?

I run after him, thrilled by the possibility that I'll finally get some answers.

I FOLLOW MYRON PAST THE GROOMING STATIONS.

He stops in front of a large supply closet in the back of the grooming area.

"In here," he whispers. "Hurry. You don't want to be seen out on the floor. They have spies everywhere."

"Who are they?" I ask.

He checks that we're not being watched, then he unlocks the door and urges me to follow him inside, bolting the door behind us.

"Is it really you?" Myron asks.

"Can you understand me?"

Myron points to his ear.

"I think you're trying to talk to me," he says, "but I only hear barking. I don't have the device for my ear."

What kind of device is this guy talking about?

I whine in frustration, a thousand questions going through my mind, none of which I can ask him.

"I've been your groomer for a while," he says. "When

I last saw you, you were with a little redheaded girl and a security guard. Super wealthy. She called you Honey."

Honey?

I get a flash of memory. The redheaded girl in pink shoes runs toward me in a beautifully decorated living room.

"You have a burn scar on the back of your neck. It looks like it's nearly healed."

Healed? It was raw and oozing just yesterday. How could my body have healed the wound so quickly? I look down at my legs and notice the scratches from jumping through the window at the warehouse are also gone.

My body seems to be healing at a superfast rate.

"I'm guessing that scar comes from one of the zapper weapons you told me about. Probably zapped your memory."

What's a zapper?

"I thought there was something strange going on with some of the dogs we were seeing, but I didn't believe it until you told me your secret."

Wait . . . This guy knows who I am!

"What did I tell you, Myron? Why did I trust you?"

He points to his ear again and shakes his head.

"I think I know why you're here," he says. "You came for this."

He reaches behind a shelf and pulls out a bright yellow briefcase, which he puts on the ground in front of me.

I sniff at it, unsure of what I'm looking at.

"It's your case," Myron says. "You asked me to hold it for you. You said some day you might get into trouble, and you'd come for it. I guess today is that day."

I left this for myself?

I look at the case, and a light flashes in my eye, startling me. A lock whirs and the case pops open.

What the—

Inside the case is a brown-and-white dog collar with a pattern similar to my coat.

"That's the translator!" Myron says, looking over my shoulder. "You were wearing a collar like that the last time I saw you. It translates your voice to an earbud. Do you want me to put it on?"

"A translator? Let's do this!"

I nudge the case in his direction and lower my head.

Here goes nothing.

Myron puts the collar around my neck. It suddenly snaps into place and tightens without his doing anything.

He gasps and steps back.

"It's like it fastened itself on its own," he says.

"How is that possible?" I ask.

He doesn't respond.

"Can you understand me now?"

He points to his ear and shakes his head.

"You need the other device," he says. "The bud for my ear. You let me borrow one before."

Translator, earbud . . . I have no idea what he's talking about.

"Maybe it's in the case?" Myron asks.

I look inside the case and Myron joins me, searching the corners and even turning it upside down.

But there's nothing.

Myron looks at me, frustrated. "I'm sorry. I thought you'd know where to find it."

There's pounding on the stockroom door, followed by the sound of someone trying to open it from the outside. I react instantly, pushing the case under a shelf and slipping into the shadows.

A woman shouts from the other side of the door. "Myron! Are you hiding back there? It's not your break time."

"That's my supervisor, Dolores," he whispers. "She's very suspicious." He puts his finger to his lips, warning me to keep quiet.

"Be there in a minute!" he calls out.

"How many times have I—"

"You're not my mother!" he shouts through the door.

"If your mother had taught you better, I wouldn't have to yell at you all the time. Be out in two minutes or I'll have security pull you out!"

I can hear the woman backing away from the door, and I come out from hiding.

Myron says, "I have to get out there before she has a hemorrhage."

Myron puts the case in the trash, covering it with boxes.

"Before we go, there's one other thing. *Maelstrom*."

"Maelstrom?"

The word doesn't ring any bells.

"You told me to say that word to you. Do you know what it means?"

I shake my head.

"I'm sorry I can't help more than that," Myron says.

He unbolts the door and leads me back through the grooming grotto. Before we leave, he pulls a bow off a station and clips it to my hair.

"So it looks like I groomed you."

I catch a glimpse of myself in the mirror, a muscular dog with a new collar and frilly purple bow in her hair.

"I don't think purple is my color, Myron."

I follow Myron outside. When we get back to the main floor, I see Chance looking panic-stricken, pacing as he waits for me near Mar del Mutt.

"I thought I lost you!" he says urgently, rushing forward.

"It took us a little longer than expected," Myron says. "But look how pretty she is."

Chance stares at the bow in my hair, then at the collar around my neck.

"Where'd she get the collar?" he asks.

"Free gift with purchase," Myron says.

"But I didn't purchase anything."

Dolores comes stomping around the corner in loud shoes, heading straight for us.

"It's my boss!" Myron says. "Get Wild out of here."

"Time to go." I nudge Chance's leg, and we head for the front entrance, hurrying past the security guard and through the sliding doors to the parking lot. I glance back to see Dolores close on our heels.

"Why are we running from that woman?" Chance asks.

"I don't know, and I don't want to stick around to find out."

Chance senses my distress, and he doesn't hesitate when

I start down Lincoln Boulevard, leaving Dolores and PetStar behind us.

I cross the street and keep going, pausing only long enough to scrape the purple bow out of my hair.

"You hated it, right?" Chance asks.

"More than anything," I say. "Now let's go home and try to figure out this collar."

"I swear it feels like you're trying to talk to me sometimes," he says. Then he laughs at himself like it's an absurd thought.

WE GO UP TO CHANCE'S ROOM.

With the bedroom door closed, I stand in front of the mirror, examining the collar from every angle.

"It looks good on you," Chance says. "Don't be so self-conscious."

He doesn't understand what I'm doing, so I scratch at the collar again, craning my neck and reaching back to try and nip at it.

"Is it too tight? Too loose?"

I whine, frustrated. He studies the collar, trying to figure out what I want.

"It's a really cool collar. It's the exact same color as your fur. It's almost like camouflage."

I step back a few feet and look at myself in the mirror again.

Chance is right. The collar is nearly invisible against my fur. He flips on a lamp, and I move closer to the mirror so I can see better. When I get near the lamp, there's a buzzing noise and the bulb shatters.

"Whoa!" Chance says, jumping back.

I sniff at the lamp. The cord is blackened where I was standing.

I follow the cord back to the wall. When I get near the outlet, the buzzing noise happens again, and the lights in the room dim and come back to full strength.

"What's happening?" Chance asks.

I glance in the mirror and see the collar glowing blue. The outlet glows the same color.

I think the collar is pulling electricity from the wall. But why does it need electricity?

I feel warmth creep in at the back of my neck. The sensation is familiar, like I've felt it a thousand times before. Myron said he'd seen me wearing a collar like this, and I'm sure he was right.

I shift and the lights dim again, followed by shouts from the housemother downstairs.

"Boys! Come to the den immediately! And whoever is using a hair dryer, cut it out!"

I hear commotion downstairs and the sound of multiple sets of footsteps.

"What's happening down there?" Chance asks.

The bedroom door flies open.

"Let's go, dumb—"

It's the angry older kid who tried to steal Chance's phone in the alley last night. He's one of Chance's housemates!

I growl, prepared to defend Chance.

The boy stands in the doorway with his mouth open, looking from Chance to me and back.

"Dude, that thing has rabies. What's it doing in here?"

"You can't say anything, Bash!"

Bash smirks, eyes narrowing. "You're going to have to pay me."

Now I really hate this kid.

"Whatever you want," Chance says.

"We'll settle up later," Bash says. "Right now the witch wants us downstairs. You'd better hide that monster and get your butt down there."

He slams the door shut.

"He saw you," Chance says. "What are we going to do now?"

"Where's Chance?!" the housemother screams.

"I have to go. We'll figure out a plan as soon as I get back."

Chance runs out and closes the door behind him. A moment later, the box on my collar makes a high-pitched tone, and the blue glow fades on the collar and the wall.

I guess the charging is done. I stare at myself in the mirror, and a dozen other questions come to mind—each chasing the next like puppies running around a pen.

I think about my collar, the wounds on my body healing in record time, Myron who called me Honey and seemed to know me from a different life . . .

What does it all mean?

That's when the smell hits me, wafting up from the den, traveling up the stairs and under the bedroom door.

It's the smell of boys and fear.

Chance is in trouble!

I open the door and slip into the hall.

TWO OFFICERS IN BLUE UNIFORMS STAND IN THE LIVING ROOM.

The sight of the blue uniforms makes me angry, and I'm not even sure why. I stay hidden at the top of the stairs, watching as they talk to Chance and four older kids who live in the house.

"Why are the cops here?" one of the boys asks.

"Because Chance's farts are a lethal weapon," Bash says, and the kids laugh.

The larger of the officers clears his throat. "We're not the police. We're Animal Control officers."

"Since when does Animal Control make house calls?" Bash says, and the housemother shushes him sternly.

"A family lost their dog," the large officer says. "So we're checking all the houses in the neighborhood."

"Must be an important family, since you guys are working on Sunday," Bash says. "Maybe there's a reward?"

The housemother is intrigued, and the Animal Control officers trade looks.

"Of course there's a reward," the small officer says.

"Ten thousand dollars," the large one says.

Who would pay ten thousand dollars to get me back?

"Ten grand for telling you about a stupid dog?" Bash asks.

The officer smiles. "That's all you have to do, son. Tell us about the dog."

Chance bites his lip, and his eyes dart from Bash to the housemother and back.

"The dog's upstairs," Bash blurts out.

"He's lying!" Chance says.

"Sorry, dude. They offered me ten K."

"You suck," Chance says.

The officers look up and catch me watching them from the top of the stairs.

"There she is!" They start toward the stairs.

"Why is there a dog in here?!" the housemother shouts and falls in behind them.

I leap up, torn between my desire to run and my instinct to protect Chance.

"Leave her alone!" Chance darts in front of the officers and blocks the staircase.

"Whoa there, son. How would you feel if you lost your dog?" the small officer asks.

"B-Bad, I mean—" Chance stutters.

"Wouldn't you want someone to bring her home?"

He looks up at me and our eyes meet. I read the silent question on his face. *Should I trust them?*

I wish I knew the answer.

The large officer smiles up at me. "I can see you two have a bond. But her family really misses her, and they want her back."

My heart beats faster. *Someone wants me back.*

Myron said I came into PetStar with a little redheaded girl and a bodyguard. Could this be the family the Animal Control officers are talking about?

"Enough," the small officer says. "We have a job to do."

He reaches for Chance—

"Just a moment," the housemother says. "I can't have the boys harmed in any way."

The housemother steps forward and puts her arms around Chance.

"We have to let these men do their jobs," she says to him, and she guides a reluctant Chance off the steps.

With the path clear, the officers start toward me. I growl a low rumble in my throat, warning them.

"Easy, dog," the small officer says.

"No need to be afraid," the large one says. "Don't you want to go home?"

"Do you know where my home is?" I ask.

I stand at the top of the stairs, frozen in place as I watch them move toward me.

"Thatta girl. Just stay where you are and we'll come to you."

Chance shouts, "Run, Wild!!!"

I follow Chance's line of sight to the large officer's hand. The man is holding something behind his back, a black dowel of some kind that looks like a little telescope. I don't know what it is, but my instinct tells me I've seen it before and I should be afraid.

"Liars!" I bark, and I dart away down the hall.

"Get her!" the officer screams, and I hear the thud of boots coming up the stairs fast behind me.

I race into the nearest room and hide behind the door. The Animal Control officers run past, panting hard.

A moment later, the door opens and Bash jogs in. He does a double take when he sees me, and then he shouts, "She's in my bedroom!"

He reaches for me, and I evade his grasp. The door flies open, and the Animal Control officers rush in.

"Stand back. We'll take care of this," the large officer says.

The small officer steps in behind him and closes the door.

"Enough talk. Let's kill her and get out of here."

"Kill her?" Bash says. "I thought you were taking her home."

I thought so, too. I look at these men now, and I feel rage.

The small officer nudges his partner. "The kid heard you, genius. Now what are we gonna do?"

He watches me closely, one hand on the black dowel in his belt.

"He's a kid. He won't say anything."

"I swear I won't say a word," Bash says. "I hate that stupid dog anyway. Just let me go, and you can do whatever you want."

The officer motions, and Bash makes a break for it, running out the bedroom door and slamming it behind him.

Now I'm alone with the two officers in the room. Whoever they really are, it's clear they mean to do me harm.

The large officer snaps his dowel toward the ground, and it extends into a foot-long baton weapon, the end crackling with electricity.

"I'm guessing that's the zapper Myron was telling me about," I say.

"Don't growl at me, mutt." The small officer lifts his zapper as I prepare to leap at him.

A piercing tone explodes in my head, scrambling my brain so I can barely think. I scream, frozen in pain and unable to attack or defend myself.

"Do you hear anything?" the small officer asks.

"Sound of silence," the other says with a grin. Then he looks at me. "Don't worry, girl. The sound only stuns you, but the beam—that's gonna leave a mark."

He raises the weapon to fire—

"Wild!"

It's Chance's voice, calling to me from outside the house.

It breaks the spell of the sound, and I whirl around and dive for the closed window.

"NO!" the large officer shouts, but I'm already gone, smashing through the glass before he can fire his weapon.

I land on the roof above the porch. It's raining outside, and the cold drops hit my back, steaming as they come in contact with my overheated body.

"Come on!" Chance shouts.

He's in the driveway below, pulling out a bike with a large basket attached to the front.

I scurry across wet roof shingles, looking for a place to jump down.

I pass by a window and see a glint of silver. It's Chance's cell phone, sitting on his bedside table, forgotten. I can't let him leave without it.

"We have to get out of here!" Chance shouts, climbing onto the bike.

"Your phone—" I start to say, but then I remember he can't understand me. "Be right back!"

I smash through Chance's bedroom window and go into the house one last time.

I dive for the phone and charger, scooping them up in my mouth and gripping them carefully between my teeth.

The door flies open, and the large officer rushes into the room. I turn to the window to escape, but the small officer is already there, climbing inside.

I'm trapped between the two of them. I growl, looking for a way out of this mess.

Both officers flick open their zappers and sparks fly.

I smell the ozone in the room from the electrical field being generated by the weapons. The smell haunts my memory, sending a shiver up my back that makes my hair stand up.

The piercing tone screams in my head, and I growl from deep in my throat, warning these men to get away from me.

The small officer points his zapper in my direction, and an arc of electricity shoots out like a lightning bolt. I duck at the last second, and the bolt flies past, striking the table next to the large officer, leaving behind a smoking, blackened hole in the wood.

The large officer screams and jumps away, cursing his partner.

"My bad," the small officer says.

"I've had enough of this dog," the large officer says, and he starts to bring up his zapper.

I spin and kick him in the chest with my hind legs, hard enough to knock him backward into the small officer and send the two of them crashing to the ground.

"See you, boys."

I leap back through the window, jumping from the roof to the driveway below, and I drop the phone into Chance's hands. He looks at it, astonished.

"How did you know—"

There are shouts from inside the house.

"We have to go," I say.

I jump into the bike basket and Chance stands on the pedals, grunting with effort as he fights to get the bike moving out of the driveway and down the street.

Back at the house, I hear the Animal Control officers fighting their way through the broken door while the large officer screams into his radio: "She's escaped. We need emergency backup!"

CHANCE IS
CELEBRATING.

We race around the corner, and Chance
pumps his fist in the air and shouts, "We did it!"

My ears perk up at a sound behind us. It's the distinctive high-revving engines of Animal Control vans on the road behind us.

"What's going on?" Chance asks.

He steals a glance behind and sees what I've already heard. Two Animal Control vans skid onto the road about half a mile back and accelerate to pursue us.

"Oh no!" He bears down on the pedals, gaining a little speed, but there's no way the two of us on a bike can outrun these supercharged vans.

I look around, trying to find a dirt path, a hiding place, anything that might give us an advantage.

"Hello?"

It's a girl's voice. I sit up in the basket and look around, startled.

I don't see a girl.

"Hello?" the voice says again. "It looks like you're in trouble."

"Did you hear that?" I ask Chance.

He stares at the road ahead, all of his focus on getting us away from the vans.

"Who are you?" the girl says. "You've got some bad people after you."

I look right and left, but there's no girl. That's when I realize the voice is in my head.

"Are you talking to me?" I say uncertainly.

"Who else would I be talking to?"

"I hear your voice in my head."

"Of course it's in your head. We're transmitting on an internet channel. I don't know what kind of equipment you're using, but you broke in on my hack, so I think I deserve to know who I'm talking to."

I look at Chance, wondering if he can hear her, too. He's pedaling as fast as he can, his face tense and focused, completely oblivious to the conversation I'm having.

That's when I realize that it's the collar! Myron said it translated the signal somehow, and it powered up in Chance's bedroom—

The girl's voice cuts in again. "I can't help you if you don't tell me who you are."

"My name's Wild."

"That's your handle?"

"What's a handle?"

"Your hacker name."

"I'm not a hacker."

"Nice try. You're up in my signal," she says. "You couldn't get here without some powerful tech."

I moan in frustration. I don't know what's happening exactly, but I know this girl can understand me, so I decide to go with it.

"I told you my name," I say. "What's yours?"

"You can call me Junebug."

"That's your hacker name?"

"You ask a lot of questions for a girl being chased by security troops."

"Who's chasing us exactly?"

She takes a sharp breath, and I wonder if she's stalling for time before answering the question.

"I don't know who they are," she says. "Some kind of high-level security operation. Advanced tech. Coordinated. Maybe military."

"*Military?* Don't you mean Animal Control?"

"Animal Control? Did you escape from a circus or something?"

That's when I realize she doesn't know I'm a dog. She's hearing the voice in my head, a girl's voice, so she's assuming I'm human.

One thing's for sure. I'm not going to correct her.

"Hey, Junebug, thanks for your help. We could sure use a friend right now."

I hear her sigh on the transmission. "Friends. Yeah, I don't have a lot of those."

"Why not?"

"Long story, Wild. Not really the time for it. Besides,

I see another half dozen vans on my monitor converging on the corner of Twenty-Sixth and Montana."

"That makes eight vehicles in all. It's like a small army."

"Like I said. Military."

"The people you're listening to—have they used the name Maelstrom?"

There's a moment of hesitation on the line.

"I've never heard that name," she says quickly, but I noticed the pause before she answered. "Animal Control, Maelstrom, angry Uber drivers. I don't know who the heck they are," she says.

"So why are they looking for me?"

"It's not you. They're looking for a dog."

I'm not willing to tell her any more, so I decide to lie to her.

"Like you said before, it's a code. My hacker name is Wild, and they call me the Dog."

"Damn, I'm good!" Junebug says, and she lets out an excited whoop.

I hear tires squeal up ahead. I look at the nearest street sign. We're on Montana and Nineteenth Street, moving toward Twentieth.

"You said something about Twenty-Sixth Street, right, Junebug?"

"For sure. That's where they're waiting."

"It's a trap!" I say. "What did you mean when you said you could see my signal?"

"You're emitting a low frequency GPS signal like a car or a phone."

"But I'm on a bike. And I don't have a phone."

"I don't know what to tell you. If I can see you, they can see you. So if you want my help—"

I look at Chance sweating with exertion. I don't know how much more of this he can take. The street sign for Twenty-Second flashes by.

"We want it," I say.

"Cool," she says, and I hear keys tapping.

Chance is pedaling for all he's worth, but he has no idea he's heading for a trap. The vans behind us drop back, aware that we're moving into danger. We cross Twenty-Third Street and Chance speeds up, thinking he's getting away.

Junebug's voice is back in my head.

"There's an alley on your right after Twenty-Fifth Street. It's not on the map."

"I see it!"

I whine at Chance to get his attention, and then I nudge my nose against his right hand.

"Not now," he says, stealing a quick glance at the vans behind. "I have to get us out of here."

I nip his hand, again gesturing to the right with my snout.

"Cut that out," he says.

I lick his hand, and he looks at me and his expression shifts to curiosity.

"What are you trying to tell me?" he asks.

I position my snout toward the alley. It's ahead on the right, just like Junebug said it would be.

"You want me to turn in to that alley?" Chance asks.

I bark at him.

"This is not happening," he mutters under his breath, and he yanks the handlebars to the right, nearly toppling us over, but cutting down the alley and avoiding the unseen trap ahead.

"Good job, Chance!" I bark my approval.

"You did it!" Junebug shouts. "When you hit Washington, take a right."

Behind us, the first van shoots past the alley, jamming on its brakes when it realizes we've disappeared.

I nudge Chance's arm, indicating we should go to the right.

"Again?" he says, and I bark.

This time he doesn't argue, and he turns onto Washington, narrowly missing a car coming from the opposite direction.

"Sharp left!" Junebug shouts. "There's another alley that takes you to Douglas Park."

I nudge Chance's left hand.

"How do you know the neighborhood?" he asks.

He turns left, staying just ahead of our pursuers who are pulling onto Washington Street a few blocks back.

"I don't know how you're doing this," Chance says to me. He bikes into the park, pedaling fast down a walking path that runs across the center of the park. The rain has stopped, and there are people everywhere. They shout and jump out of the way.

"Sorry!" Chance yells to them.

"We're almost out of the park," I say to Junebug. "What's next?"

"Until we figure out where your signal is coming from,

you have to confuse them. Stay where there's a lot of inter-ference, like the high-power line that runs along Wilshire Boulevard. Take Wilshire all the way to the Promenade. Do you think you can make it that far?"

I look at Chance. He's breathing hard, but his face is determined.

"I'm sure we can," I say. "What happens when we get to the Promenade?"

"You go where the electronic interference is the loudest."

"Where's that?"

"The Apple Store."

WE ABANDON THE BIKE AT THE ENTRANCE TO THE PROMENADE.

Chance seems like he's in shock, but I can't tell if it's from being pursued all over Santa Monica, or because I was giving him directions. He locks up his bike, then stares at me wide-eyed.

"Can you understand me, Wild?"

There are strangers all around us, and I'm afraid to draw any attention, so I play dumb, sniffing the ground and looking this way and that.

"I'm so confused," Chance says. "Sometimes you act like a regular dog, and sometimes— What are you?"

What am I?

A street drummer starts a set nearby, the rhythms played loudly on overturned white buckets. I look at the hundreds of people on the Promenade, and I realize we'd better keep moving.

Junebug told me to go to the Apple Store. She got us out of the jam with the so-called Animal Control vans, so I don't see any reason to distrust her advice now.

I look at the map of the Promenade and head south, giving Chance a bark to come with me.

"This is crazy," he mutters, and he follows along.

The Apple Store is a huge, glass-fronted arch the size of an airplane hangar.

"What are we doing here?" Chance asks.

"I wish I knew." I bark, and he opens the door for me.

The smell of electronics hits me, and I rear back, uncomfortable.

"What's wrong?" Chance asks.

There's something familiar about the smell. Not the Apple Store itself, but the scents of technology—warm aluminum, computer chips, and the wires that connect them. I get a memory flash of a laboratory ringed by computer equipment.

For a second, it feels like I might remember something important—

"A dog and his boy," a blue-shirted Apple employee says. "It's like a heartwarming commercial come to life."

Chance looks at me and rolls his eyes.

"Considering becoming part of the Apple family?"

"I already have a family," Chance says.

"Got ya," the employee says, backing off. "Feel free to browse, and enjoy the free Wi-Fi."

I follow Chance toward a table of shiny new phones. The smell of the technology is still making me uncomfortable, but whatever memory was brewing seems to be gone.

"My mom said she'd buy me one of these for my birthday," Chance says. "That was last year, right before things got bad. Maybe this year will be different."

He turns on a phone, opens a browser, and types: *If you find a lost pet.*

I put two paws on the table and look at the row of shiny new phones with bright, colorful screens. I can see why humans find these cool. One of the screens shows kites flying through the air. I lick my lips, wanting to chase after them.

"They're not real," Chance says when he notices me pawing at the screen.

"I know, I know," I say.

I look back at the screen, and the kites disappear, replaced by a girl's face. I blink hard, startled by the sudden change. The girl is maybe thirteen years old, with a dark complexion and light green eyes. She has long black hair with a cool blue stripe down one side.

It seems like I'm looking at a still photo, and then the girl moves, surprising me.

"Hi there," the girl says.

Chance looks over to see who's talking.

"On the screen," the girl says.

I recognize the girl's voice. It's Junebug, the girl I heard on the bike.

I stare at her, wondering why it feels like there's something familiar about her face. I comb my memory, trying to figure out if I've met her before.

"Are you on a video chat or something?" Chance asks.

"Put the girl on," Junebug says.

"What girl?"

"Are you the guy with the blue-van dudes after you?"

Chance's face goes pale. "How do you know about that?"

"Just put her on."

Chance looks around us. "There's no girl."

"The one they call the Dog."

Chance glances down at me, then he points the phone toward me. "You mean this dog?"

"Listen, kid—"

"I'm not a kid."

"You're pretty young," Junebug says.

"So are you."

Junebug scowls. "I don't have time to fool around. The blue dudes are still after you, they just can't see your signal inside the store. But they'll figure it out pretty fast, and they're super angry."

"How do you know all this?" Chance asks.

"Let me talk to the girl I was talking to earlier. Her handle is Wild."

"Wild is a dog," Chance says.

Junebug's mouth drops open. "You mean the Dog is a real dog?"

"What else would she be?" Chance asks.

"But I've been talking to her."

"That's impossible," Chance says. "She can't talk."

"Hang on a second," Junebug says, and she pulls out an earpiece of some kind and slips it into her right ear.

I remember the moment that Myron pointed to his ear in the backroom at PetStar. *I don't have have the device for my ear,* he said.

Junebug taps her earpiece. *Is that what he meant?*

"Hello? Can you hear me?" she asks.

I hear her voice in my head, just like I did when I was on the bike.

"It's me," I say.

She gasps. "You're Wild? But you're a dog!"

"I think we established that."

"How are we talking to each other?"

"I think it's my collar," I say. "It's some kind of translator."

Chance rubs his face in disbelief. "This is impossible," he says. "Are you talking to Wild?"

"This is surreal," Junebug says.

"I hear you speaking, but I only hear Wild barking," Chance says.

"Wild says it has something to do with her collar," Junebug says.

Chance stares at me, and his mouth drops open.

"That's like Nobel Prize stuff," Chance says.

"I didn't invent it. I'm just wearing it," I say.

Junebug laughs, and Chance frowns. "What are you guys talking about?"

"She said something funny."

"It's not fair that you can talk to her and I can't. How did you figure that out?"

"I'm a hacker," she says with a shrug.

"But you're my age."

"I got you out of the jam on your bike, didn't I?"

He looks from me to Junebug, confused. "You were talking to her during the chase?"

"Explain what happened," I tell Junebug.

She starts to tell him, while I check the area to make sure we're still safe.

I trot over to the glass storefront, just in time to see the large Animal Control officer from the group home walk by with some kind of device in his hand. He scans the Promenade in front of the store, his head turning this way and that as he looks for my signal.

I growl at him through the glass, wanting to get back at him for trying to shoot me in Chance's bedroom. But I restrain myself and back up so I can watch him through the legs of customers without being seen.

He turns the device toward the Apple Store, then he frowns and adjusts the dial. I can see from his face that he can't find my signal. It seems like he's going to keep moving, but then he changes his mind at the last minute and heads toward the door.

I race back to find Junebug and Chance in mid-conversation.

"What kind of name is Junebug?" he's asking her.

"A totally cool name."

"I hate to break up the party, but we've got company. There's an Animal Control officer walking into the store."

"Darn it. Hold on." Junebug swivels in her chair and types at a keyboard. "Wild saw one of the blue dudes," she explains to Chance. "I checked the radio comms. He hasn't seen you yet. You have to get out of there!"

"Where are we going to go?" Chance asks.

"The beach," Junebug says.

Chance frowns. "It's not really a beach day."

"You're not going for a tan, kid."

"Stop calling me that."

"There's a major power line that runs up Ocean Avenue," Junebug says. "If you stay on the beach and west of the avenue, they won't be able to see you."

"I get it," I say, and I pull at Chance's pant leg.

The large officer is on the far side of the store. There are dozens of people between us and him, but it's only a matter of time before he finds us.

"Before we go," Chance says to Junebug. "How do I talk to Wild like you do?"

"No time," she says.

Junebug cuts off the chat, and the screen goes black. I see the large officer turn in our direction.

We have to go!

I dart through the customers' legs, staying low so I won't be seen as Chance and I rush out of the store.

THE RAIN HAS STOPPED.

I feel a cool breeze blowing in from the ocean as Chance and I blend with the tourists walking along the Promenade. I check over my shoulder, looking and listening for trouble.

"Is he back there?" Chance asks.

I sniff the air and decide we've lost him. I yip to let Chance know we're okay, at least for a moment.

A group of stroller moms block the way ahead. They're watching a street performer making balloon animals.

I pause, fascinated, as the performer twists a long, thin balloon, transforming it into the shape of a dachshund.

I dash forward, wanting to grab the colorful balloon.

"Whoa!" Chance says, pulling me back by the collar. "What happened to keeping a low profile?"

"Sorry. I don't know what came over me." I snort and shake it off.

The performer hands the balloon dog to a little boy who

squeals in delight and clutches it to his chest. The boy presses too hard and the balloon pops, causing the dog to deflate.

I bark my displeasure.

"It's just a balloon," Chance says. "You can't get upset at little stuff like that. My mom says if you let the little stuff get to you, what will happen when the big stuff comes around?"

I guess he's right. The noise, the balloons, the people. It's a little too much for me after the shock of being understood for the first time by Junebug.

I turn away from the crowd, and Chance guides me off the Promenade and across Ocean Avenue. We walk south along the edge of the beach until the crowds thin out. Chance finds a bench hidden behind a bank of trees that faces the water.

He slumps down, exhausted, and I hop up and sit next to him. I push my face into the wind and feel it tickle across my lips. It sends a ripple of pleasure through me.

"I always like it when my mom takes me to the beach," Chance says.

He's sitting with his head back, letting the sun warm his face. I guess humans enjoy the beach, too.

"Sunday is our phone-call day," he says. "I'm supposed to talk to my mom in an hour and a half. What am I going to tell her about all this, Wild?"

He bites his lip, thinking hard.

"And what if my housemother reports that I'm gone?" he says.

I don't think she's going to do that, but I can't explain it to Chance. Not yet, at least.

I look at his eyes, heavy with concern, and I'm frustrated again at not being able to speak to him.

Myron said I loaned him an earbud that allowed us to talk. That means there's an earbud somewhere that would allow me to talk with Chance. But where?

I think about the discussion of the collar that we had in the Apple Store, and I nudge Chance.

"What is it?"

I turn to the side, exposing the collar for his inspection.

"Junebug said you thought the collar was translating your voice."

I bark an acknowledgment.

"Is it okay if I touch it?"

I lower my head, granting him access to the collar.

"This is where it was glowing earlier," he says, tugging at the section on the back of my neck. "It feels like one solid piece, except it gets thicker in the back here."

I crane my neck, trying to see what he sees.

"There's some kind of indentation. . . ."

I hear a mechanical swish from the back of the collar, and Chance gasps.

"It opened!" he says. "There's something in here."

"What?" I say excitedly.

He holds out his hand, palm open. There's a tiny white earbud in his hand, much smaller than the one Junebug was wearing.

"The box on the collar had a hidden chamber. When I took out the earbud, it closed again."

It's the second part of the translator Myron was talking about!

I frantically wiggle my ears, then point my snout toward Chance's head.

"You want me to put it in my ear?" Chance asks nervously.

I nod. Chance moves the tiny bud around with his finger.

"What if it's dangerous?"

I whimper and nudge his calf.

Be brave, Chance.

He takes a deep breath. "I'd try anything to talk with you."

He pinches the white bud and slides it into his ear, then scrunches up his face as if he's in pain.

I watch him, concerned.

A moment later he relaxes, opening and closing his jaw a few times. "It hurt for a second, but now I'm okay. So what do we do next?"

"I don't know. Maybe there's some kind of volume—"

Chance screams and jumps up from the bench. "I heard a girl's voice in my head!"

"What girl?"

He looks at me, his breath quickening. "What girl? It's you, Wild!"

Oh. Right.

"You can understand me?"

"Yes! It's amazing! Junebug was telling the truth!"

I skitter back and forth excitedly while Chance hops up and down laughing.

"This is great!" I say.

"We can talk to each other. This is the most amazing invention ever!"

Some people on the beach look over. I imagine them seeing a boy and his dog, jumping up and down for no reason at all.

"We can't attract too much attention," I say.

"You're right," he says, struggling to hold back his excitement. He paces in front of the bench. "How is this possible? Who made something like this?"

"I don't know who made it or where it comes from," I say.

He stops suddenly. "So wait. Have you been able to understand me since we met?"

"Sure."

"You speak human language and dog language?"

"I can understand dogs, but they don't have much to say. It's basic, like one-word sentences and a lot of noises."

"Just like Bash in the group home."

Chance is funny, even more so now that we're talking to each other.

"Something like that," I say with a laugh. "But dogs don't rely on language like people do. For us it's more about smell and our other senses."

"Not you, though. You're special. How did you become like this?"

"That's what I'm trying to figure out. I'm not just a dog, and I'm not human. It's like I'm stuck somewhere in between."

He sits down next to me on the bench, suddenly serious.

"You must know where you came from. I mean, where do you live? Where's your family?"

I shake my head. "I woke up on a yacht, and my mind was blank. It's like my memory was erased when I was shot."

"Shot?"

"That mark on the back of my neck. I think it's from those zapper weapons the Animal Control officers were carrying."

He looks at the fur on the back of my neck. "The mark is gone."

"My body seems to heal really fast. That's something else unusual about me."

"Can you remember your name?" Chance asks.

"I don't remember anything."

I don't tell Chance about the dreams of the blond soldier or the flashback of the little girl in pink shoes. I don't want to frighten him.

"Wow," Chance says. "I thought the group home was weird, but this is like next level."

He leans back, shaking his head in disbelief. "What's it like to be a dog?" he asks.

"I don't know exactly. What's it like to be a human?"

He thinks about it for a second. "It's not like anything. I'm just who I am."

"Me, too."

"Wow. I never thought of it like that."

I sit next to him, and both of us get quiet. I listen to the waves crashing against the sand. It's amazing to think I was in that same ocean less than forty-eight hours ago, swimming for my life.

I hear laughter carried on the wind. I look out at children playing in the waves. They splash water at each other as their parents watch from the beach nearby.

My heart feels heavy. "I have to find out who I am. Then maybe I'll know where to find my home."

"I want to go home, too," Chance says quietly. "I guess we've got something in common."

He takes out his phone. "No signal out here," he says. "My mom's going to call in a little while."

"We'll figure it out," I say.

He kicks at the sand, then he glances up at the laughing children.

"I'll help you find your home, Wild. I just need to get to the court hearing with my mom on Thursday. I know that's a few days away, but those Animal Control guys are coming after us hard, and we can't go back to the group home—"

Chance sniffles, and he quickly covers his face with his hands.

"Sorry," he says through tears. "You must think I'm a loser."

His crying opens up something inside me, and I want to run to him, lick his face, press my body against his until his sadness goes away.

But I don't do it.

I'm not even sure I know how. I'm not one of those cute, cuddly dogs that can make people feel better.

What kind of dog am I?

"Hey, Chance." He sniffles and looks up. "I'll get you back to your mom."

He watches me through bloodshot eyes. "Really?"

"I promise."

He rubs his face, and his tears stop. Then he clears his throat and stands up. "I was thinking about that Magic Myron guy. He knew something about you, didn't he?"

"That's right. I trusted him in the past, but I don't know why. He had a case with my collar in it. He told me I left it for myself."

"Did you leave anything else? Like money so we can get a hotel and some room service?"

Room service. I remember that term. I get a memory of thick steaks served on silver trays.

"No money," I say. "Only this collar. And a few clues from what Myron said."

"If Myron knows about your past, shouldn't we go back and talk to him? Especially now that I can translate for you. You can ask him whatever you want."

"That's a smart idea," I say. "But Junebug warned us to stay near the beach, or the Animal Control guys will be able to see my signal."

"*Your* signal. But I don't have a signal." Chance points away from the beach. "I could go back into town and talk to Myron without you."

"It's too dangerous. Plus, I don't think he'd talk to you alone."

"That settles it, then," Chance says. "We have to go together."

I don't like the idea of Chance coming with me, but we can't stay here forever, and I'm not willing to leave him alone with an army of Animal Control officers looking for us.

So I choose the best of the bad options in front of me.

"We'll go back to PetStar," I say.

"YES!" Chance smiles and pumps his fist.

"We have to stay under the power lines, move fast, and dodge the officers. Can you handle that?"

"I've been dodging bullies for three months," he says. "I can run really fast."

"WELCOME TO PETSTAR, WHERE YOUR PET IS THE STAR OF THE SHOW."

A young woman in a red vest smiles and greets us at the front of the store.

"We're looking for Myron the groomer," Chance says.

The woman's smile drops.

"Oh, um, just a moment. I'll have to—"

She takes out a radio.

"Ask her what she's doing," I tell Chance.

"Who are you calling?"

A moment later, the supervisor from earlier comes around the corner in loud heels. She's whispering into her cell phone, so I turn an ear in her direction.

"I think it's the Nine," she says. "Yes, I understand, sir."

What is the Nine?

She hangs up and approaches us with a fake smile.

"I'm Dolores. How can I help you today, young man? And young dog?"

"We're looking for Magic Myron."

Dolores and the greeter exchange glances.

The greeter says, "We have other groomers on staff who—"

"Myron is our favorite," Chance says. "He gets along with my dog really well."

"Myron isn't working today," Dolores says.

But we saw Myron this morning.

I exchange looks with Chance. "Ask her when we can come back," I say.

"Could we make an appointment for another day?" Chance asks.

Dolores taps her heel nervously.

"I'm afraid he'll be gone for a while," Dolores says.

"Let's get out of here," I tell Chance.

"We'll come back another time," Chance says, expertly picking up my cue.

Chance and I speedwalk toward the front of the store.

"What's going on?" he asks.

"I have a bad feeling."

We pass the kind security guard who was on duty earlier. He motions for us to come over.

"You're looking for Myron, right?"

"He's our favorite groomer," Chance says.

"He's everyone's favorite. But he had an accident."

"What kind of accident?" Chance asks, surprised.

I hear the squeal of brakes outside the store and the sound of a heavy vehicle stopping too quickly.

"The kind you shouldn't ask questions about," the guard says through gritted teeth.

He leans toward us and his voice drops to a whisper.

"You have to get out of here. They pay people in the store to spy for them."

"Who pays them?" Chance asks.

Before the guard can answer, the PA system crackles.

"Attention, customers, the store is closing. Please exit through the back immediately."

Confused pets and owners make their way to the back of the store.

"Why the back?" Chance asks.

"I warned you," the guard says, and he walks away.

"Let's go out the front," I tell Chance. "Right now."

Chance follows me through the door, and I let out an involuntary yelp.

The parking lot is filled with blue Animal Control vans in a large semicircle facing the front entrance of PetStar. Dozens of AC officers wait by the vans, using them for cover. Most of them have black zappers in their hands. The air sizzles with electricity.

"Back inside!" I shout to Chance.

I turn and see Dolores locking the door behind us, then running into the depths of the store.

"I knew I didn't like her," I say.

"The guard was telling the truth about the spies," Chance says.

I look at the multiple vans surrounding us. I don't think there are this many Animal Control vehicles in all of Los Angeles County. Who are these people, and what do they want from us?

In the rear of the parking lot the commander of the Animal Control officers stands on the roof of a blue jeep.

"Stay where you are," she announces through a megaphone.

"How did they find us so fast?" Chance asks.

"Dolores made a call when she heard we were there."

I think it's the Nine, sir.

"You're surrounded," the AC commander announces. "Walk slowly toward the officers and you won't be harmed."

"Do you believe her?" Chance asks, panic in his voice.

I look at the zappers and remember what happened at the group home.

I don't answer Chance because I don't want to scare him, but I know one thing for sure. We have to get out of here.

I scan the parking lot, trying to find an escape route. There's a tight cordon of officers, their trucks parked nose-to-nose, blocking every exit. If I were alone, I might be able to dodge their weapons and leap over the vans, but I have Chance with me, and I can't risk him getting hurt.

"There's nowhere to go," the commander says. "You have to surrender."

On the edge of the parking lot, a black Honda Accord sideswipes an Animal Control van and races into the center of the cordon. Its horn beeps as it heads straight for us.

I bark loudly to warn Chance, and he screams and jumps back.

The Accord swerves at the last second and screeches to a

stop barely a foot in front of us. The passenger side window is open.

"Get in!" a girl shouts.

"It's the girl from the Apple Store!" Chance says.

Sure enough, Junebug is in the driver's seat, blue-striped hair shining in the sun.

"Hop in the back," Junebug shouts, and she revs the engine.

The commander roars into the megaphone. "You in the car. Throw the keys out the window and exit the vehicle."

"Come on!" Junebug says. "We gotta Command-Option-Escape."

"What do we do?" Chance asks me.

I don't fully trust Junebug, but she seems like our best option right now.

"Get in!" I tell Chance.

Chance throws open the back door, and I leap into the car. He jumps in behind me and a second later we're in motion, Junebug pressing the gas and accelerating through the parking lot, heading straight for one of the Animal Control vans.

"Put on your seat belts!" she says.

Chance quickly snaps himself in and puts a seat belt over my shoulder.

"We're gonna crash into that van!" Chance shouts.

"Oh, please," Junebug says, and she jerks the wheel at the last second, squeezing into a narrow space between two vans, so tight that the Accord scrapes both bumpers and sparks fly.

"So much for my dad's insurance premiums," she says.

We burst through the cordon, jump a curb, and land hard on the street beyond the parking lot. The tires skid and catch asphalt, and Junebug slams the gas, shooting up Lincoln Boulevard as we make our escape.

THERE'S SOMETHING FAMILIAR ABOUT JUNEBUG'S FACE.

I look at her and feel the same déjà vu I felt the first time I saw her on the phone in the Apple Store.

"Have we met before?" I ask her.

"I have one of those faces," she says. "I'm a mutt. Everyone thinks they know me."

She turns the corner like a pro and the tires squeal. How did a young girl learn to drive so well?

Chance must be having similar doubts because he leans over and whispers, "Do you think we can trust her?"

"I don't know yet."

"I can hear you both," Junebug says, tapping her earpiece. "So you might want to gossip about me offline. Speaking of which, it looks like you guys figured out how to talk to each other. Congrats."

I look at her strange earpiece, not at all like the tiny white earbud Chance found in my collar.

"Where did you get the device you're wearing?" I ask her.

"It's my own design," Junebug says. "I use it for spoofing military communications. When it crossed your signal, we started talking, and I thought you were one of them. That was before I knew you were some kind of super dog."

"I'm not a super dog."

"Says the dog who's speaking like a human."

"Wild's special," Chance says. "That's why Animal Control wants her."

"Animal Control? Are you kidding?" Junebug says. "Two dozen vans surround a PetStar in a coordinated capture. That sounds like a military operation to me."

"Why would the military care about Wild?"

He looks at me, hoping I might have the answer. But I have none to give.

"What do you know about these vans?" I ask Junebug.

"I know what you know," she says. "I stumbled into this, same as you guys."

Chance looks worriedly through the back window. "Let's find a way to stumble out."

"Hello? Can I at least get a thank-you? I scraped up my dad's new car to save you guys. Now I'd like to drop you off and go on with my day."

She cuts left and right, expertly navigating through busy afternoon traffic.

"We don't have a destination," I admit.

"You're running?"

"For now."

She sighs. "I get it. Listen, then, I'm thinking the highway is our best bet. Clear out of the area as fast as possible."

"Fast sounds good," Chance says.

"The highway it is. Thanks, Junebug," I say.

"Finally, a thank-you." She slams the gas, accelerating up Lincoln Boulevard.

"Hey, how old are you?" Chance asks.

"I'm thirteen," Junebug says. "But I'll be fourteen soon."

"Me, too," Chance says. "We're too young to have a permit. How can you even drive?"

"My dad taught me. I'm homeschooled."

"Homeschooled? What's that like?"

"Take the worst of school and the worst of home and put them together."

"Yikes," Chance says.

"Yeah, my dad is my teacher and my principal."

"At least the principal taught you how to drive," Chance says.

I hear a cacophony of horns behind us, followed by the familiar sound of the vans in pursuit.

"They're onto us," I say.

"We'll be at the ramp in ten seconds," Junebug warns. "Hang on."

She mounts the ramp at high speed, jerking over to the breakdown lane to bypass the cars waiting in line. The tires squeal as they fight for traction on the tight curve.

Junebug alternates the gas and brake in perfect coordination, keeping us on the ramp for a critical few seconds until she hits the highway and barrels forward on a straightaway.

"I don't feel so good," Chance says.

Junebug frowns. "Don't barf in my dad's car, kid."

"I'm not a kid."

"Then don't barf."

Chance grumbles and gives her the evil eye.

"How did they find us again?" I wonder out loud.

"Same way I found you at PetStar," Junebug says. "You've still got that GPS transmitter on you."

"Is it your collar?" Chance asks me.

"Not possible," I say. "We saw the van in the alley that first time before I even had the collar."

"But you're not wearing anything else," Chance says.

"Bad news," Junebug says. "If she's not wearing it, it's gotta be inside her."

"Inside her body?" Chance asks nervously.

My heart pounds as I think about some kind of device being inside me. How did it get there? And how do I get it out?

"Check under her skin," Junebug says. "Look for bumps or small scars where something may have been implanted."

"I can't do that," Chance says quietly.

"Why not?"

"She hates being touched."

"She's your dog," Junebug says.

"She's not my dog," Chance says. "She's her own dog."

"Please look for it," I tell Chance. "It's okay."

Chance gently puts his hands on either side of my head by my ears. He runs his hands down my neck, and I shiver as a ripple of conflicting emotions moves through me. His touch is comforting, but it also triggers alarms inside. My instinct warns me to attack before he can hurt me.

"Try to relax," Chance says, sensing the tension in my

body. I take deep breaths, doing my best to relax beneath his touch.

He completes an entire pass down my back, then he checks my tail.

"I'm not finding anything!" he says.

"They'd probably plant it as far away from her collar as possible to prevent interference," Junebug says.

"Maybe check my rear legs. And hurry. The vans are back," I say.

"I don't hear them," Chance says.

"Look at your ears, and look at mine."

"Good point."

"Less talk, more action," Junebug says.

Chance presses at various places over my legs and hindquarters. After a moment, he stops and doubles back over my right hip.

"I think I found something. There's a hard patch under her skin."

"Let me feel it," I say, and I twist around, licking the area where Chance is pressing. I find a thin line of scar tissue from a past incision.

My throat goes dry as I realize Junebug was right.

"It's inside me," I say.

"How do we get it out?" Chance asks, his voice high and afraid.

"Do you have a knife?" Junebug asks.

"No, and I left my surgical kit at home, too," Chance says.

"I only have my laptop," Junebug says.

"Maybe we can drive to a vet clinic," Chance says.

I hear multiple vans behind us, their high-charged engines distinct from the other vehicles on the road.

"The vans are close," I say. "We're out of time."

"I don't know what to do," Chance says, panicking.

My stomach lurches as I realize what needs to be done.

"Move your hand and sit back," I tell Chance.

When he lets go, I lick along my hip, finding the scar. Then I twist around and chew at my fur.

"No way!" Chance says, horrified. "You're going to hurt yourself, Wild."

"What's she doing?" Junebug asks.

"You don't want to know."

I bite down, ignoring my disgust, and get a fang into my skin. I feel a sharp pain as my tooth pierces the flesh, followed by a burning sensation as I bite down and open a small cut above my hip.

"Now I'm really going to throw up," Chance says.

The taste of my blood fills my mouth, firing off recollections of my battle with Thunder, and deeper things from my past, violent acts that sit on the edge of my memory.

I yelp and come back to the present, fighting to focus on the task in front of me.

The chip. I have to get it out.

I lick at the wound, and my tongue connects with a small square of silicon implanted on my hip muscle. I get a tooth under it and feel it lift from the tissue beneath it.

I spit it onto the seat in front of me.

"She did it!" Chance says.

I look at the microchip, a tiny black box with metal

probes on one side where it was attached. I flip it over with my nose, and I see something printed in the corner, a word so faint it's almost imperceptible: BREEDX.

"I've got you," Chance says. He presses a T-shirt against the wound, applying pressure to stop the bleeding.

"What's happening back there?" Junebug says.

"I found a Girls Who Code T-shirt to use as a bandage."

"My favorite T-shirt!"

"It's just a shirt," Chance says. "Don't cry about it, kid."

"Not funny," Junebug says.

Chance grins and throws me a wink.

Suddenly the inside of the car lights up, and I hear the sound of rotor blades above us.

"Is that a helicopter?" Chance cranes his neck out the window.

I don't need to look. I can hear the helicopter above us, and my eye picks up the spectrum of laser light they're using to mark our car.

"Animal Control doesn't have friggin' helicopters!" Chance shouts.

"I told you it's not Animal Control," Junebug retorts. "Get rid of the chip!"

Chance snatches up the BreedX chip and flings it out the window. It bounces across the pavement before it catches in the wheel of a truck and goes flying over the guard rail into the opposite side of the highway.

"It's gone!" Chance says.

The van engines slow behind us, adjusting to the position of the chip. But the helicopter stays locked on target.

"They're tracking us from above with a laser," I say.

"Not for long," Junebug says. She pulls off the highway and parks under the metal canopy of a busy gas station.

The helicopter lingers for a moment, then the glow in the car disappears and the helicopter veers away above us, following the chip.

"Are they gone?" Chance asks.

"Doesn't make sense to stay on us if the chip shows we're somewhere else," Junebug says.

"You're good at this stuff," Chance says.

"Thanks for the compliment," she says. "Keep 'em coming."

"You both did a great job," I say. "Now let's get some bandages."

"And some food!" Chance says. "But wait. I don't have any money."

"I have money," Junebug says with a sigh. "By the way, you guys would make terrible fugitives."

She pulls out of the gas station, tires squealing as she gets us far away from trouble.

WE'RE SITTING BEHIND A 7-ELEVEN.

Chance is next to me on the curb, both of us out of sight from the road, waiting for Junebug to buy food and medical supplies. Chance leans over me and applies pressure to the wound. The bleeding has stopped, but he's worried, and there's something nice about the attention and the way he wants to care for me.

"I'm so hungry," Chance says. "I hope Junebug buys—"

His phone vibrates and he sits up, startled.

"It's her!"

"Who?"

He yanks the silver cell phone from his pocket and answers the call.

"Hey, Mom," he says into the phone.

I see joy and relief flood his face as he hears his mother's voice. His happiness is infectious, and I find myself getting happy, too, sniffing at his legs and prancing around his feet.

"I'm not doing anything," Chance says. "Just hanging out." He holds a finger to his lips to warn me not to bark.

An *LA Times* blows around the parking lot, scattered by the wind. The local section glides past and sticks on the curb in front of me. A headline catches my eye, and I stop to read it.

"LUXURY YACHT SINKS OFF CATALINA ISLAND"

> A mega-yacht belonging to the billionaire heiress Helen Horvath sank off Catalina Island Friday. The cause of the accident is yet to be determined.

I look at the photo of the yacht and instantly recognize it as the ship I woke up on.

Helen Horvath.

The name sounds familiar, and it triggers fragments of memory and emotion, a little redheaded girl playing in a massive living room with marble walls.

"How's everything at the treatment center?" Chance asks over the phone.

I read more in the article.

> Ms. Horvath and her family, who were not on board at the time, had been staying at their summer residence in Malibu.

Is it possible the Horvaths are my family? Why else would I have been on their yacht?

Junebug comes around the corner, and I let the paper go, watching it blow away across the parking lot. I'd rather not tell her what I've found out, at least not until I know her better.

Junebug looks at Chance on the phone and throws me a quizzical look.

"It's his mom," I whisper.

"What if he gives us away?" she asks.

"That won't happen."

Chance walks toward us, still on the phone. "Hey, did you hear anything from the group home?"

He listens for a minute.

"No, everything's fine," he says. "I just wondered if they called you."

He looks over and gives us a thumbs-up.

"Okay, Mom. I'll see you Thursday. I swear I'm fine. Nothing to worry about at all. Love you, too. I can't wait to see you."

He hangs up and I see tears in his eyes.

"Whoa, what was all that about?" Junebug asks.

Chance wipes snot from his nose and turns away, trying to hide his tears.

"Sorry I asked," Junebug says.

I walk over to Chance and whine until he looks down at me.

"I'm okay," he says. "I just miss her a lot."

"What did she say about the group home?"

"They haven't called. I thought the housemother would report me missing."

"She won't do that," I say.

"Why not?"

"They probably paid her to keep her mouth shut. Those soldiers are trying to find us. They don't want everyone else looking for us at the same time. Too messy."

"So nobody is looking for me?"

"Nobody you want to find you," Junebug says, interrupting. "Now let's get you cleaned up, Wild."

She opens a bag and pulls out antiseptic, paper towels, and a small sewing kit.

"Sorry in advance, but this is going to sting a little."

She pours antiseptic on my wound to clean it out, then she threads a needle.

"Do you have a favorite color?" she asks.

"I like my color," I say. "Can you make it match?"

"I'll do my best."

"You know how to give someone stitches, too?" Chance asks.

"Welcome to the wonderful world of homeschooling," Junebug says. "End result? I can do stuff."

"Weird stuff. Doesn't your dad teach you anything normal?"

"This is normal for him."

Junebug places the first stitch, and I don't make a sound.

"You're a tough dog," Junebug says as the needle passes in and out of my skin.

"All dogs are tough," I say. "But maybe I'm extra tough."

The stitches hurt a little, but they're nothing compared to jumping through windows and fighting strange dogs.

"What kind of chip did you find inside?" she asks.

"A transistor of some kind. There were prongs going into my muscle."

"My dad owns dogs. That doesn't sound like a regular dog chip to me."

"I think we've established that I'm not a regular dog."

"Good point," she says, "but it's not like you put a chip inside yourself. Were there any words or numbers on it?"

"There was a name. BreedX."

She hesitates, then places the next stitch. "I've never heard of it."

"I've heard of it," Chance says proudly.

Junebug glances up. "You're full of surprises."

"It was some kind of cool dog-breeding company. My mom promised we could get a dog a couple of years ago, so I was looking around online. I remember their website was pretty high-tech, but I don't remember much else."

"I can do a search later, maybe find out who registered the domain and trace them back—"

She looks up to find Chance and me staring at her. She finishes the last stitch and breaks off the thread.

"What's with you guys?"

"I know you're homeschooled and all," Chance says, "but you're a hacker, you can drive, perform first aid—how can you do all this stuff if you're only thirteen?"

"My dad's an even bigger freak than I told you," Junebug says. "He's a scientist and also a doomsday prepper."

"Like a survivalist?" Chance asks.

"How do you know the term?" Junebug asks.

"I know stuff, too. But it's mostly from watching Nat Geo."

"Anyway, that's my dad. He thinks the end of the world is coming, and he wants me to be able to survive under any conditions, so he teaches me all this stuff."

"Wow. Homeschooling sounds cool," Chance says.

"It's not cool," she says quietly. "I wouldn't mind if I never went home again."

Chance's expression darkens. "Me neither," he says. "Or at least, not back to that group home. I want to be with my mom."

"Yeah, what was all that on the phone before?" Junebug asks.

"Long story," Chance says, and he bites at his lip.

Junebug looks over at me. "Seems like you're both trying to get home."

I stand up and shake off the dirt from the sidewalk.

"We appreciate all of your help, Junebug. But Chance and I are going to go our own way now."

"We are?" Chance asks.

"But, wait," Junebug says. "I bought snacks and everything. I figured you guys must be hungry."

"I'm hungry," Chance says.

"Nothing against you, Junebug. But like you said, you risked a lot to help us, and you already banged up your dad's car. I don't want to get you into any more trouble."

"I crashed a security cordon. I'm already in trouble."

"Not really. You can fade into the background, erase your tracks online. That's not a stretch for a hacker like you."

"Good point." She sighs and brushes dirt from her pants. "Whatever. If you guys don't want me around anymore, I get it."

"I kind of want you around," Chance says. "You're weird, but in a good way."

"Listen, both of you. These soldiers are not playing." I turn to Chance. "I think we should let Junebug get back to her father, and you and I can hide out until it's time to take you back to your mom."

Junebug nods. "I get it, Wild. So I guess this is good-bye."

Chance kicks a stone against the curb and frowns at me. He's obviously upset, and he's terrible at hiding his feelings.

"I don't think you're a kid," she tells him.

"You don't?"

"Nah, I think you're a tough guy."

Chance laughs and stares at the ground. "I think you're a tough girl."

"Thanks for the compliment."

She turns back to me. "You're the first talking dog I've met. I won't forget you."

"And you're the first thirteen-year-old I've met who drives like a race car driver."

She takes out the Accord keys, and suddenly a police car shoots around the corner and stops between us and the Honda. A Culver City police officer gets out and walks toward us.

Junebug and Chance freeze, surprised by his sudden appearance. I adjust my body to look like the friendly dogs

I've seen on the street—head up, tail wagging. I could be anyone's pet.

"How are you kids doing this morning?" the cop asks.

"We're okay," Chance says cautiously.

"Are you Windward students?"

"Culver City High," Junebug says. "But it's Sunday, our day of rest. Also our day of Spicy Cheetos."

The cop smiles. I'm amazed at how easily Junebug lies to him.

"All right, then," the cop says. "By the way, anyone know whose car that is?"

He's pointing at the Accord.

"It's my dad's car," Junebug says.

The cop's posture stiffens.

"Do you have your father's permission to use it?"

"As long as I'm home before dark," Junebug says.

"I ran the plate from across the street. This car was reported stolen in Westlake Village a day ago."

Junebug's composure cracks for the first time. I can smell her fear mixing with Chance's.

"That's not right," she says. "I'm allowed to use the car."

"No need to get upset," the cop says. "Let's head down to the station and we'll sort it out."

Across the street, one of the blue vans rolls by, the driver's head on swivel. I'm guessing they found the BreedX chip on the highway and realized what happened. Now they've sent the vans out to look for us.

The driver sees us with the cop at the 7-Eleven, and he stops on the corner, engine idling.

"I need you to get in my car," the police officer says.

I think about our options. Should we go with the police officer or risk it out on the road, pursued by the police *and* Animal Control—or whoever they are?

"Listen," I say to the kids. "We'll go with the police and let Junebug sort things out with her dad. We're safer in a police station right now than we are on the road."

The kids nod imperceptibly.

"Does your dog have a cough or something?" the cop asks.

"She's just getting over a cold," Chance says.

"Let's get going," the cop says. "I'll let the dog ride in the back with you if you promise not to give me any trouble."

"Thank you, sir," Chance says.

"I can't lose my laptop or my dad will kill me. It's in the Accord," Junebug says.

"Don't worry. I'll get it for you."

The cop opens the back door of the squad car. I smell a combination of gun oil, sweat, and old french fries.

We climb in, and the cop closes the door, then goes to retrieve Junebug's laptop.

"Did you steal your dad's car?" I ask Junebug.

"It was more of a borrowing situation," she says. "And he tends to overreact." Her head drops, and she leans over with elbows on her knees.

"I thought my family had problems," Chance says.

The cop slides into the driver's seat and starts the engine.

JUNEBUG SQUIRMS IN HER SEAT.

I sense her agitation, and it concerns me.
Scared people do stupid things, just like scared animals.

"Relax," I tell her. "This will work out."

"I can't relax," she says, and she taps hard on the partition, trying to get the cop's attention.

"I'm sure this is a mistake, Officer."

"I'm sure it is, too," the cop says. "We'll give your dad a call at the station and get it all sorted."

Junebug looks at us apologetically.

"I told you, my dad's a maniac," she whispers. "He said if I ran away again, he'd have me arrested. I thought he was bluffing."

"You ran away?" Chance asks.

"I told you already. I heard you guys were in trouble, and I came to your rescue."

"How is that running away?"

"I didn't tell him I was leaving."

"Or that you were taking his car," I say.

Junebug shrugs. "He's usually not paying that much attention. Not to me."

The cop calls into the station, reporting that he has two minors in custody and he'll arrive in five minutes.

He leans back to talk to us.

"When we get to the station, I'll put you in a room to chill out, and we'll call your parents and social services."

I smell the sweat break out under Chance's arms.

"If they call social services, it might affect the hearing," he whispers.

"What do you mean?" Junebug asks.

"I have to go to Family Court with my mom on Thursday."

"Sounds rough," Junebug says.

"It's going to be okay," I say, concerned that the kids are getting overly upset. "They'll release Chance and me when they find out we have nothing to do with the car, and they'll release you when your father vouches for you."

"If he vouches. He might want me to spend some time in juvie so I learn my lesson."

"I'm totally screwed," Chance says.

The cop's cell phone vibrates. "Now who's this calling?" he says.

He answers the phone, and I sense his energy change. He speaks quietly and glances at us in the rearview mirror multiple times.

"Roger that," he says abruptly, and he ends the call.

We turn a corner, and the Culver City police station comes into view. The cop drives right past the entrance and keeps going.

Junebug throws me a *What's up?* gesture.

"Something's wrong," I say.

"Wasn't that the station?" Junebug asks.

The cop doesn't respond. I tense, my body warning me of impending danger.

"Where are we going?" Chance asks.

"Different station," the cop says.

"Which station?" Junebug demands.

"Too many questions," the cop mutters under his breath. He seems upset, and he refuses to look back at us.

Who did he speak to on the phone?

The cop turns south, and the houses get smaller and more run-down.

"I've got a bad feeling," Chance says.

"I think he's heading for the Ballona Wetlands," Junebug whispers.

"What are those?" Chance asks.

"Isolated marshes near the ocean," Junebug says.

"Isolated? That doesn't sound good at all," Chance says.

I'm looking around the backseat, frantically searching for a way to escape. I press on the rear window, wondering if I can force my way through, but I feel the thick layers of wire-reinforced glass. We're in the back of a police car that has been designed to prevent escape.

"We're in trouble, aren't we?" Junebug asks me.

"Give me a minute to think—"

Chance grabs for Junebug's hand. Their fingers entwine, knuckles white with tension.

The hackles on the back of my neck stand up, my instincts on high alert.

This is my fault. If it wasn't for me, these kids wouldn't be here right now. They'd each be having a quiet Sunday at home, safe and sound.

"I'm going to get us out of this," I say.

"But how?" Chance asks.

The cop stops at the light, and I hear the roar of a truck engine close by. I look to our right and see a large black-and-red truck with a lightning bolt painted on the hood barreling toward us.

I watch for a moment in disbelief, certain it will slow down or swerve to avoid us. But it does the opposite, speeding up on a collision course with the police car.

"Hang on!" I scream.

I barely get the words out before the truck hits us at full speed. Metal grinds against metal and glass shatters. For a few seconds the patrol car is airborne, and then it crashes down hard, rolling over on itself, flinging us violently from side to side.

I hear the children screaming, but there's nothing I can do to help or protect them. *This is my fault,* I think again, as the crash seems to go on forever. We spin end over end, until suddenly we're upside down, and the world goes black.

I OPEN MY EYES.

A saintly woman in robes looks down at me from above, a golden light shining from around her head. She reaches out, beckoning to me.

Come home.

I blink hard and realize I'm awake and looking at a religious painting on the wall.

Where am I?

There's a soft bedroll on the floor beneath me. I feel music vibrating from somewhere nearby, the electronic beats of Korean pop music. I hear a mix of accents as people talk and laugh. The delicious smell of cinnamon and roasted tomatoes fills my nose.

I sit up on my haunches and feel pain everywhere. That's when I remember the police car crashing, and the screams of the children. My body stiffens in fear.

Where are the children?

There's a gauze curtain hanging from the ceiling across

the room. The sound of gentle snoring emanates from behind it.

I stand on unsteady legs and pull the curtain aside. Chance and Junebug are sleeping under the covers of a large bed. There's a bandage on Chance's head, expertly wrapped. Junebug's face has some scratches, but otherwise she looks unharmed. The reinforced cage of the police car must have kept us safe in the crash. But how did we get here, and who helped us?

I listen at the door and hear the music change to Spanish rap. I glance back at the kids, trusting they'll be okay for a few minutes while I figure out what's going on.

I take the doorknob in my mouth, concerned that it will be locked, but I turn it and it opens.

We're not prisoners here. So what are we?

I step into the hall, ready for anything.

THE HOUSE SEEMS TO BE EMPTY.

I follow the voices down the hall until I emerge in a kitchen. Trays of raw meat are sitting on the counter. I lick my lips involuntarily. The music is louder here, and I can smell more meat sizzling on the grill outside. I push through the screen door into an enclosed backyard.

It's twilight now, and colored lights are strung from the trees, giving everything a festive glow. I see a mix of people in the yard, old and young, all of different ethnicities and speaking different languages. I wonder what they're doing together back here. A woman with long gray hair stands at a grill cooking rows of succulent meat.

Is this a party of some kind?

I stay in the shadows, trying to understand what I'm seeing.

"Are you hungry?"

I spin around to find a young woman with kind eyes

smiling at me. She has a tray of freshly grilled meat in her hands, and I can't help but lick my lips again.

"Of course you are," she says, and she picks some pieces from the tray and puts them on the ground at her feet. "Korean short rib. Very delicious."

I hesitate, remembering my track record with strangers and food.

"It's okay," she says. She takes a bite of food from the tray, showing me the meat is safe.

Still, I'm in no rush to take food from a stranger.

I see several tough young men in T-shirts and jeans standing around the edge of the yard. They face out toward the street, not inward toward us.

They must be guards. *But what are they guarding?*

A man steps out of the house and freezes in his tracks when he sees me. We stare at each other across the yard.

It's Ruben, the dogfighter who tricked me the other night.

"Secreta. It's nice to see you again," he says.

I notice a nasty black-and-blue mark over one of his eyes and scratches on his face like he's been roughed up. I remember him saying people would hurt him if he didn't bring a dog to fight. Now I wonder what happened to him after I left.

I growl as he comes toward me.

"I'm not going to hurt you," he says.

Regardless of what happened to him, I still don't trust this man. I rush forward, teeth bared, threatening—

A little girl comes running around the corner, flinging herself against Ruben's leg.

"Papa! Pick me up!

"It's a bad time to play, *Mija*."

He watches me.

"Please, Papa!"

He lifts her to his chest for a hug, watching me the whole time. He speaks to me over the girl's shoulder.

"I don't know how exactly, but I think you can understand me. There are kids here. They have nothing to do with this business between us."

I look at Ruben holding his daughter, and I back up a step, not letting down my guard, but no longer advancing.

He puts the little girl down in front of him.

"Go to Grandma," he says to the girl. "She'll give you something good to eat."

The girl scowls, but she consents. She rushes toward the kitchen, pausing next to me as Ruben stiffens.

"Good doggy," she says, and her hand darts out and pats my head—once, twice, a third time. Then she laughs and skips away.

The fruity smell of her skin lingers in my nose, and I'm overcome by the memory of a different child. I'm snuggled against the redheaded girl who is petting me with long, gentle strokes across my back. I look down and see her pink boat shoes—

I shake my head and flap my ears, dispersing the girl's scent, and the memory along with it.

"Maybe you'll sit down and have some food with us," Ruben says.

"You fooled me once before. It's not going to happen again." I move toward him, snarling. The people in the yard gasp and back away.

"I know you're angry. I tricked you, and I used you. That's the kind of person I am. Heaven help me, I'm not a good man. Not when my back is against the wall and I have people to care for."

He gestures around the yard.

"I don't know if you can understand what a family is, Secreta. Maybe it doesn't matter to you."

"I understand everything, but I'm not about to feel sorry for you," I say.

Ruben looks at me strangely.

"I wonder what you would say if you could talk. I've been looking for you for two days now. Ever since you blew through that warehouse window and ran away. I knew you were special, and I knew I had to find you."

He takes a step toward me, emboldened.

"You got a lot of blue vans after you, girl. I've had some trouble with Animal Control in my time, but I don't know who these blue-van *vatos* are. I only know there's a lot of them, and they want you bad. Why is that?"

I growl, warning him back, but he continues to walk forward, speaking to me in a soft voice.

"I saw you and the kids get picked up by the cop. I watched him drive past the station, and I knew you were in trouble. That's why I got involved. I owed you one. Maybe more than one."

That's when I understand.

It was Ruben's truck that hit us.

"I have a proposal for you," he says. "At the very least, I think you'll want to hear it."

The kitchen door opens behind me, and Chance and Junebug's scents mix with the many odors in the backyard.

"What's going on?" Chance asks. "It looks like a party out here."

He rubs his eyes, adjusting to the scene. Junebug is behind him, equally confused.

"Welcome to the family," Ruben says.

Junebug looks around at the Latin, Asian, and Black faces around us.

"Whose family is it?" she asks.

"That's what we call ourselves," Ruben says. "As long as you're in this neighborhood, you're under the protection of the family, and those blue vans can't get to you."

He gestures to family members and drifts toward the table to arrange plates of food.

I move to the kids, turning my back on Ruben so he doesn't see me talking.

"How do you feel?" I ask.

"I feel like I got hit by a truck," Junebug says.

"No kidding," Chance says. "Who are these people?"

"They're some kind of organization. I don't know the details yet."

Ruben motions us toward a picnic table in the center of the yard. "Please come and sit with me. You need to eat, and I need to talk to you about Secreta."

"You mean Wild?" Chance says.

"Is that her real name? I call her Secreta."

"If you already have a name for her, that means you've met her before, right?"

"We met for the first time a couple of days ago."

"Do you know where her home is?" Chance asks.

"She doesn't live with you?"

Chance shakes his head. "We're following the clues, trying to find out where she's from."

Ruben nods. "So that's what this is all about."

He motions to the table where the family lays out plates heaped with food. The children hesitate, standing back with me.

"Why did you save us from the cop?" Junebug asks.

"I'm not a fan of cops, except my brother Eduardo in San Diego. He's a detective, but he's the black sheep of the family. More importantly, I owed Secreta a big favor."

He picks up a chicken wing and digs in.

"Come now. The food is safe, and we have a lot to discuss."

Chance crouches by my side and whispers, "Why does he talk to you like you can understand? Does he have an earbud?"

"No earbud. I think he's spent a lot of time with dogs, and he can sense that I'm different somehow. Let's keep our secret, okay?"

"Got it."

"Me, too," Junebug says.

I walk over and hop up on the picnic bench, and Chance and Junebug sit on either side of me.

"Hey, do you have Wi-Fi here?" Junebug asks. "I need to do a little research."

Ruben leans across the table and shows her the network. Then he goes back to the chicken wings on his plate, so I take some chicken, too. Chance and Junebug follow my lead and dig in.

Ruben watches us for a moment, giving us an opportunity to get some food down, and then he starts to speak.

"The family and I, we work together as part of a certain business enterprise."

"Dogs," Junebug says.

Ruben's eyes widen in surprise. "Sharp girl."

"I saw bags of dog food and veterinary supplies in the kitchen cabinets," Junebug says. "Kind of strange when there are no dogs."

"The dog thing was a temporary—" His face turns red as he clears his throat. "It was stupidity on my part. I got involved in something I couldn't handle."

"Dogfighting is illegal," Chance says.

"It was more like dog wrestling," Ruben says.

Junebug slams her fist on the table. "Call it whatever you want, but it's unethical."

Ruben sighs and gestures toward the dozen or so members of his family standing around the yard.

"I was just trying to take care of my people."

"But what about the dogs?" Chance demands.

Ruben frowns. "I agree, it's not an excuse. Anyway, those days are over. I left the kennel gate open by mistake, and the dogs ran away. One of them pooped on my pillow before he left."

ALLEN ZADOFF

Junebug chuckles, and Ruben cracks a smile.

"Serves me right, huh? Anyway, Secreta—I mean Wild— is something special. I knew it the first minute I saw her. What she did the other night—it was amazing. I saw her fling a huge rottweiler across the room like he weighed nothing," Ruben says.

Junebug and Chance look at me, amazed.

"Then she bounced around like a Super Ball, jumped twenty feet in the air, and smashed through a window."

"She's a cool dog," Junebug says quietly, "but she's not going to wrestle for you. We won't let her."

"I don't want her to wrestle. I want her to work."

I sit up, surprised by what I'm hearing.

"Work how?" Chance asks skeptically.

"Maybe we start a YouTube channel and show her doing tricks. Or maybe we create some kind of stage show. I think people would pay a lot of money if they could see what she can do."

"You want to put her online?" Chance asks. "But people are looking for her."

"We'll dye her fur and give her a new name."

"Doesn't sound like a good idea to me," Chance says.

Ruben motions beyond the yard to the neighborhood around us.

"You can't run forever, Wild, especially with these kids. They're in danger because of you. You know I'm telling the truth."

My breathing quickens as I listen to his words. I can try to dismiss what he's saying, but I know he's right. I only have

122

to think back to the moment in the police car when I realized we were trapped.

"You said you were looking for her home," he tells Chance. "Maybe you've found it. Right here."

We sit silently as a sad Spanish ballad plays behind us.

I scan the faces of the family members around the yard. They smile and their postures are warm and open.

Could I be a part of this family?

"Maybe there's nothing out there for you," Ruben says. "Or maybe you'd be better off not knowing what's out there."

For just a moment, I remember the blond soldier screaming in my nightmare.

"I don't know who you were," Ruben says. "But I know who you can be. With us."

I look at Chance and Junebug, and I feel the connection to them I've built up in only a short time. I think about going through a day without the sound of Chance's voice or the scent of him by my side. The idea makes me sad beyond belief.

"Thank him for his offer," I say, "but I won't do it. I'm not leaving you alone."

I hop off the bench and walk away. I hear Ruben sigh deeply behind me.

"She made her decision," Chance says.

"That's a shame," Ruben says.

In a moment he's on his feet and whistling to the family members, who begin to gather together.

"What's happening?" Junebug asks.

"I can't keep her against her will. I've seen what she can

do," Ruben says. "So we're going to help you with some supplies. Food, clothes. A car, too."

"What about my dad's Honda?"

"The car back at the 7-Eleven? Kiss that thing goodbye. My people saw them towing it away to the police impound lot."

WE WAIT TOGETHER IN FRONT OF THE HOUSE.

A big white BMW pulls up with Ruben at the wheel.

Junebug whistles at the shiny new car. "That's my kind of upgrade."

Ruben hops out and the family members load up the back of the car with backpacks of food and bottles of water.

"That's everything you'll need for a few days," Ruben says. "Now, who does the driving in this group? Wild is special, but she has paws."

"I'm the driver," Junebug says.

"But you're a kid," Ruben says.

"In your face," Chance says with a grin.

"I'm a young adult," Junebug says. "Besides, it's LA. There are kids driving expensive cars all over the place."

"Good point." Ruben tosses Junebug the keys.

She hops in the driver's seat while Chance and I climb into the back.

"Thanks for everything," Chance says.

"Be careful," Ruben responds. "Those blue vans are everywhere around the city. Once you leave this neighborhood, you're on your own."

"We can deal," Chance tells him.

Ruben throws us a final wave and heads back into the house with the family.

"What are we going to do now?" Chance asks nervously.

"You said you could deal," Junebug says.

"I was bluffing!"

"I have an idea," she says. "I used the Wi-Fi at Ruben's place to do a little research on BreedX."

"What did you find?" I ask.

She passes her laptop to Chance. I glance over his shoulder and see the browser open to an article called "The Dog Days of BreedX."

"Tomorrow's Dogs Today," Chance says. "I remember now. That was their motto."

"That's right," Junebug says. "BreedX claimed they were creating hyperintelligent dogs that would be perfect family pets."

"Hyperintelligence. That explains a lot. Maybe I'm a BreedX dog."

"Do you recognize this woman, Madeline Pao?" Junebug asks.

I look at the picture of a young woman in a lab coat beaming with pride in front of a pack of dogs. I'm hoping for some flash of memory, but it doesn't come.

"She was the founder of BreedX," Junebug says, "but she was discredited by the scientific community."

"Why?" Chance asks.

"Because the company never delivered a dog."

"What about me?" I ask.

Junebug shrugs. "The company failed at its mission, and it was dissolved. BreedX doesn't even exist anymore."

"But I exist, and I had a BreedX chip inside me. How is that possible?"

"We should just ask Dr. Pao," Chance says.

"Bingo," Junebug says. "I did a tax-records search and she's living in Hidden Hills."

"That's in the Valley," Chance says. "What do you think, Wild?"

I look from Chance to Junebug, their eyes wide and excited at the idea of another adventure.

"I think our next stop is Dr. Pao's house."

DR. PAO'S COMPOUND IS AT THE END OF A LONG ROAD.

It's surrounded by high brick walls covered with snaking vines to keep it safe from prying eyes.

"The doctor sure likes her privacy," Junebug says.

We've left the BMW on a nearby street and walked to the compound, hoping we might talk our way inside. But now we're standing in front of an imposing steel gate with no buzzer or intercom.

"What's that black ball?" Chance points to a pole with a black orb on the top.

"It's a security system," Junebug says. "Probably a motion detector of some kind."

She waves her hand in front of the orb, and a second later I hear a click followed by a woman's voice, high and anxious, through a speaker.

"Who's there?"

Junebug smiles. "Hi, we're selling cookies for a school project."

"Go away," the woman says.

"Please, Dr. Pao—"

"How do you know who I am? Get off my property."

Junebug pouts and backs off. "So much for being charming."

"Tell her you found a BreedX dog," I say.

"Let me try," Chance says, and he steps up to the orb. "Dr. Pao, we found a BreedX dog, and we really need your help."

"BreedX? That's impossible."

Chance motions me forward. I hop up on my back paws and press my snout to the orb.

"We're in trouble," Chance says to the doctor. "We need your help."

"What kind of trouble?"

"We're not totally sure, but there are blue vans after us and—"

The steel gate groans and opens.

Chance gives Junebug a look. "Pretty good, huh?"

THERE ARE GARDENS EVERYWHERE.

The property is much bigger than it looks from the outside, and there are lush gardens between us and the house. We walk past a vegetable garden covered in chicken-wire fencing, then a flower garden with rainbows of color, then small groves of fruit trees in neat rows. The air is thick with the smell of ripe and rotting citrus fruit.

There's life all around us, but no dogs. Not that I can smell at least.

Are we in the right place?

Far back on the property is a large Spanish-style home with big windows. As we approach, the front door opens, and a skinny woman with short-cropped black hair peeks out.

"You're just children," she says.

"Young adults," Junebug says.

"Are you Dr. Pao?" Chance asks.

"She's not on a leash," the doctor says, glaring at me.

"She doesn't need a leash," Chance says. "She's well-behaved."

"If she makes a move toward me—"

"She won't. I promise," Chance says.

Dr. Pao cautiously steps out of the house and closes the door firmly behind her. She stands on the stoop looking down at us.

"Approach slowly so I can get a good look at her," she says.

We take a few steps toward the doctor, and she holds up her hand.

"Close enough."

She studies my face and body for a long moment. Then she shakes her head.

"She's not one of mine. Sorry you came all this way for nothing."

"I thought you didn't breed any dogs," Junebug says.

The doctor stops, and her face turns red with anger. "Do you believe everything you read on the internet?"

"Tell her about the chip," I say.

"We found a chip inside of her," Junebug says. "It had BreedX printed on it."

"Prove it," Dr. Pao says. "Show it to me."

"We had to throw it away," Chance says. "We were being tracked."

"I don't believe you," the doctor says, but her face tells a different story. She's flushed with fear.

"We're telling the truth!" Chance says. "She still has a big hole in her leg."

I turn to the side, and Chance points to the place where Junebug sewed me up at the 7-Eleven. I look back to find the skin has healed, and the stitches have fallen out.

"It's gone!" Chance says. "That's impossible."

Junebug looks, too. "How could it heal so quickly?"

"The chip was right here," Chance says. "I swear."

The doctor looks upset, her eyes darting from Junebug to me and back again.

"What do we do now?" Chance asks me.

"Tell her we just want to sit down with her and—"

"Were you talking to the dog?" the doctor asks, her voice on the edge of panic.

Chance is too slow with his denial, and without warning, Dr. Pao jumps off the stairs and disappears around the back of the house.

"Follow her!" I shout, and we take off after her.

The doctor is faster than she looks, and the yard is like a maze that thickens as we move deeper into it. We run through paths overgrown with trees, scraping past branches and leaping over thick roots that grow up out of the soil.

I only want to question the doctor, but she's running from us like her life depends on it. We nearly catch up with her when she leaps over a hedge, racing toward a barn hidden in the rear of the property.

I speed up, outpacing Chance and Junebug and gaining on the doctor. She makes it to the barn a split second before me.

She flings open the door and races inside. I leap from

twenty feet away and hit the door, pushing it open and tumbling inside after her.

The scent of dogs hits me full in the face, and my eyes instantly adjust to the low light inside the barn. The interior of the building is a kennel, and there are more than two dozen labradoodle dogs staring at me. They seem nearly identical, crossbreeds with big friendly faces and curly hair.

Dr. Pao wades into the center of the pack, and the dogs shift to let her through, then close in around her like they're trained to protect her.

What kinds of dogs are these, and how are they communicating?

I edge forward and sniff at the pack. They react instantly, tightening the circle around the doctor.

My heart quickens with excitement at the idea I might have found my pack. "Are you the BreedX dogs? I'm not here to hurt you or the doctor."

They don't respond.

"Can you understand what I'm saying?" I ask, still hopeful.

They bark at one another, passing messages in a language more sophisticated than normal dogs', but far less sophisticated than human language. I hear barked warnings to be cautious and reminders to protect the doctor from outsiders.

It's obvious they can communicate with one another, but they can't speak to me.

I turn away, disappointed.

The barn door flies open, and Chance and Junebug run in, breathless.

"Whoa," Chance says. "They all look alike."

"And they're cute!" Junebug says.

"Stay back," I warn them. "These aren't regular dogs."

"Are they like you?" Chance asks.

"Not like me, but not normal. They're protecting Dr. Pao. She's hiding behind them in the shadows."

"Dr. Pao!" Chance shouts. "We're not trying to hurt you."

"We just want to talk," Junebug says.

Dr. Pao shouts a command from somewhere in the barn, and the formation of dogs separates and splits down the middle. Dr. Pao walks forward, and we approach through the pack to join her.

The doctor looks up. I see tears glistening on her cheeks. *Why is she crying?*

"I thought you were them," she says.

"Who?" Chance asks.

"Maelstrom."

"Are they after you, too?" Junebug asks.

"I need to know what Maelstrom is," I tell Chance.

"We heard the word *Maelstrom* before, but we don't—"

The doctor cuts him off. "You talked to the dog again, didn't you?"

"Tell her the truth," I say.

"Her name is Wild," Chance says. "She told me to ask you about Maelstrom."

Dr. Pao's eyes widen. "In human language?"

Chance nods.

"Oh my gosh. They've done it. They've broken the language barrier."

Dr. Pao comes toward us with the natural curiosity of a scientist overcoming her fear.

"I only heard barking," Dr. Pao says. "How can you understand her?"

"There's a translator in her collar," Chance says, "and I can hear her through a special device in my ear."

"Don't leave me out," Junebug says. "I've got a device, too."

Dr. Pao looks from Junebug to Chance and then to my collar.

"Come to the house with me," she says. "There's a lot we need to talk about."

"YOU DON'T REMEMBER ANYTHING?" THE DOCTOR ASKS.

We're in Dr. Pao's living room, and she's on the sofa across from me wearing the earpiece that Junebug loaned to her. One of her labradoodles is by her side, and she runs her fingers through the dog's curly hair.

"I don't remember much," I say. "Flashes of training, blue uniforms, and a yacht."

"A yacht?"

Chance perks up behind me. He's across the room with Junebug, drinking juice and eating snacks.

"I woke up on a sinking ship," I tell Dr. Pao. "I saw an article in the *LA Times* yesterday saying a yacht belonging to Helen Horvath sunk last week."

"Horvath? The rich woman who's constantly in trouble?" Chance says.

"You've heard of her?" I ask.

Junebug shoots Chance a quizzical look. "She's surprised I've heard of Helen Horvath," Chance explains.

"Everyone's heard of her," Junebug says. "She's rich and beautiful, and people think she's shady because she gives away a ton of money from her foundation."

"What's so shady about that?" Chance asks.

"It's not the money, it's who she chooses to give it to," Dr. Pao says. "Her foundation has been under investigation for a while."

"I don't know anything about her or her foundation," I say. "And I have no idea why I was on her family yacht."

"Very mysterious," Dr. Pao says.

Her labradoodle hops off the couch, walking toward Chance and Junebug.

"Oh my god, I'm having a cute attack," Junebug says, and Chance rolls his eyes.

"Is it okay to play with her?" Junebug asks.

"Her name's Maddie," Dr. Pao says. "She's very friendly, and she loves kids. Wait until you see what kind of tricks she can do."

The big labradoodle happily eats chips from Junebug's hand while Chance scratches behind her floppy ears. Maddie seems like she's in heaven, oblivious to the conversation around her. I try to imagine what it would be like to be a normal dog, to live with that kind of freedom. . . .

Who am I kidding?

I'm not a normal dog. I have to find out what kind of dog I am so I'll know what to do next. I turn away from Maddie and the children.

"I need to know about BreedX," I tell the doctor.

"It was my life's work and my passion," she says, her

ALLEN ZADOFF

eyes bright. "I wanted to create the greatest pets in history."

Across the room, Junebug squeals with laughter as
Maddie squats down and nudges Junebug onto her back,
galloping around and snorting to imitate a horse.

"I told you she knew tricks," Dr. Pao says.

"I want to try, too!" Chance says, and he trades places
with Junebug. He shouts with pleasure as Maddie lifts him
into the air and prances around the room.

"You see what I mean about creating great pets?" Dr. Pao
says. "But BreedX wasn't just about fun. We were practical,
too. It started with the idea of service animals. Drug-sniffing
dogs, guide dogs . . . Imagine a family pet who could detect
if your children were using drugs, who could tell if you were
getting sick when your scent changed, who could keep your
family safe crossing the street in traffic. All of this without
much training, because it would be bred into the dog."

"One dog could do all of those things?"

"Those capacities already exist in different breeds,"
Dr. Pao says. "But I found a way to merge them into one
optimized animal. A BreedX dog would have the qualities
of a working dog combined with the sociability, loyalty, and
friendliness of a family pet."

"Like Maddie!" Junebug says, pulling the labradoodle
onto her lap.

"Exactly," Dr. Pao says.

"But the article online said you never delivered any dogs,"
Chance says.

Dr. Pao's face goes red with anger. "I couldn't deliver
them because General Rupani stopped me!"

138

"Who stopped you?" I ask, sitting up and cocking my ears.

"His name is General Rupani. He's head of a supersecret arm of the military with the codename Maelstrom."

"Finally!" Chance says, and he leans forward, all attention on the doctor. Junebug shuffles nervously behind him.

"Rupani," I say, trying to remember the face that goes with the name, but nothing comes to me.

Maddie senses the doctor's distress and disengages from Junebug, trotting across the room and planting her head on the doctor's thigh. The doctor runs her fingers through Maddie's fur.

"Two men in uniforms showed up at our offices," Dr. Pao says. "They said the military would like to license our technology for a pilot program."

"But you didn't go along with it," I say.

"Absolutely not. My dream was to create next-gen pets, not the next generation of—"

She looks at me, her voice trailing off.

"Of what?" I ask. I sense she's going to tell us something vital—that I'm close to finding out who, and what, I am.

"I'm sorry," Dr. Pao says. "I lost control of myself for a moment."

I whine, frustrated.

A movement outside the window draws my attention. I look at a bank of trees beyond the compound. I watch the branches swaying for a few seconds, and I decide it was just the wind.

I look back at Dr. Pao. She seems tired, her face older than it was a few moments ago.

"I said no to those soldiers," she says. "But that wasn't the end of it. I had no idea who I was really dealing with."

"Maelstrom," I say.

Dr. Pao's face goes dark.

"You keep saying that word. What is it?" Chance asks. We're all listening intently.

Dr. Pao stands up. "I'd like to speak to Wild alone."

"No way!" Chance says. "I'm never going to find out what that Maelstrom thing is!"

"Give us a couple of minutes," I urge Chance. He pouts and relays the message to Junebug.

"Bummer," she says.

The kids leave the room, and Dr. Pao closes the door firmly behind them.

"I haven't told you the whole story," she says. "And you need to know."

DR. PAO STANDS WITH HER BACK TO THE DOOR.

"Before we get into this," she says, "I have to ask how well you know that girl."

"Junebug? Not very well, but she's been a huge help. We wouldn't have made it this far without her."

Dr. Pao points to her ear. "Junebug's device doesn't match the boy's."

"Hers is homemade."

"Homemade? Your collar and earbud—that's Maelstrom technology. How could a kid make a device that emulates their tech and translates your voice?"

"She's a hacker. She creates all kinds of things, and she stumbled onto my collar transmission. It was a coincidence, Dr. Pao."

"That seems unlikely."

"What are you trying to say?"

"Maelstrom started with my tech, and they've developed it even further in the years since. Even if she's a brilliant hacker, she's still just a kid. There's no way she could replicate their work."

"Then how would she get her hands on it?"

"That's exactly what I'm wondering. Be careful around her, okay? Now, let's talk about you."

She walks across the room and unlocks a drawer in her desk. She removes a folder and puts it on the table in front of me.

I hop up on two paws and look it over.

It's a complex diagram of dog breeds, colors, and lines crisscrossing hundreds of breed names.

"This is a genomic map of the family of dogs," Dr. Pao says. "It lists every trait and the breed from which it arose. And with CRISPR—"

"What is that?"

"Gene-editing software. CRISPR technology allows us to make precise changes in the genes of animals."

I scan the page, frightened by the implications of what's in front of me.

"You're saying you can mix and match traits to create the dog you want in the lab?"

She nods. "Like a recipe. We can include certain ingredients and exclude others."

She turns to a second page. It's the same diagram, only now large sections of the circle are blacked out and others are highlighted.

I scan the highlighted qualities on the diagram: courage, intelligence, cleverness, cunning, aggression, and more.

Something isn't making sense to me.

"But these qualities exist in many breeds, don't they?"

"Like I said, my specialty was combining different traits into a single breed. This is a recipe for one animal, turned up to one hundred percent. An animal that could fit in anywhere, that would be intelligent enough to understand her surroundings, that would have hyper-aggressive instincts that could be unleashed at will. A super-breed."

"This is what BreedX was working on?"

She shakes her head. "These aren't BreedX documents, Wild. They're from Maelstrom."

I look at the chart and I shiver, the fur on my neck standing up.

She says, "The soldiers brought me these documents. This is what they wanted. It's the dog I refused to create for them."

"They wanted you to breed a weapon."

She closes the folder.

"When I refused, they stole my company and destroyed my reputation."

"Then they continued your work on their own."

"As far as I can tell, they've been refining and developing multiple generations of dogs. Who knows how far they've gotten."

She locks the folder in her desk and turns back to me.

"Actually, we know how far, Wild. Because I'm talking to you."

My fur stands up as fear creeps down my skin.

"I'm not a . . . I had a BreedX chip under my skin," I say. "That makes me a BreedX dog. Like Maddie."

I say the words, but they ring hollow. The doctor shakes her head sadly.

"I wish that were true. The only BreedX dogs that exist are the ones I made later. My intelligent labradoodles like Maddie. Like I said outside, you can't be one of mine."

"Then why did I have a BreedX chip inside me?"

"We developed an advanced locator chip. Maelstrom is probably using some of my original tech. It's cheaper than making it from scratch."

"So if I'm not one of your dogs—"

"You're one of theirs."

I blink hard as I remember the copper taste of blood in my mouth, and the rage that filled me with the desire to kill.

Dr. Pao kneels down next to me, her voice gentle. "I can't know for sure. But if you are and they spent all that time and money to create you, why do they want to destroy you?"

I remember my nightmare, and in my mind I hear the blond soldier screaming, blood soaking through his uniform.

"I think I'm a threat to them," I say.

"You said you have no memories, only some impressions."

"But they don't know that, do they? They left me for dead, and here I am walking the streets."

I turn away from her and look at my reflection in the window.

"My memory is starting to return. I'm having nightmares about a soldier."

"A Maelstrom soldier?"

"I believe so."

I hear the soldier scream, and it sends a shiver through me.

"I think I did something terrible," I say.

I shudder from snout to tail, then I turn away from my reflection, away from the memories.

"You've been more than helpful, Dr. Pao, but I think we should go now."

She nods. "I'll return the earpiece to Junebug."

She pauses at the door.

"After talking to you, it's safe to assume that the Animal Control officers are actually Maelstrom agents."

"That's what I've been thinking, too."

Animal Control is Maelstrom. That explains the mysterious vans, the officers desperate to get me—at any price.

"It's the perfect cover story," Dr. Pao says. "They can't have soldiers running around the streets in broad daylight, but Animal Control officers? They claim there's a wild dog loose, or an outbreak of rabies, and they can go anywhere without raising suspicion."

"They're not going to stop, are they?"

The doctor reaches for the door, then hesitates, lowering her voice.

"Maybe the children should stay here."

"I understand there's some danger. But Maelstrom is after me, not them."

"It's not Maelstrom I'm worried about."

She turns away from the door. Maddie trots over to her side, and the doctor strokes her behind the ears.

"You're not a pet, Wild. You're a weaponized animal, bred for intelligence, bred for strength and violence."

"I would never hurt those kids."

She takes a deep breath and kneels down, meeting my gaze.

"You might not be able to help yourself," she says.

An explosion shakes the house, setting off a piercing siren.

"It's the perimeter alarm!" Dr. Pao shouts.

She flings open the doors, and I see Chance and Junebug running toward us, unharmed.

"They're breaking through the wall!" Dr. Pao says.

She's looking at a video monitor on the desk, and I can see a large group of uniformed soldiers entering the compound, black zapper weapons held at their sides as they spread throughout the grounds.

Junebug grabs her earpiece from Dr. Pao and puts it in.

"What's happening out there?" she asks.

"It's Maelstrom," I say. "They found us."

"They must have been watching the house," Dr. Pao shouts. "We have to get you out of here!"

WE RUN THROUGH THE YARD, USING THE TREES AS COVER.

Another explosion knocks us to the ground, and the rear wall of the compound shatters in front of us.

I call to Chance, but he doesn't respond. He's dazed, rubbing at his ears where the pressure wave hit him. I grab the back of his shirt and pull him behind a thick tree trunk. A blue armored vehicle smashes through the bricks and advances into the yard, crushing flowers beneath its tracks. Maelstrom soldiers dressed as Animal Control officers stream into the opening in the broken wall behind it. There are dozens of them, their faces set hard, zapper weapons drawn and at the ready.

Junebug is a few feet away with Dr. Pao and her dog Maddie, the three of them crouched behind thick hedges. I raise my paw in warning, signaling them to keep quiet.

The Maelstrom soldiers stop just inside the ruined wall line, waiting for orders. All at once they extend their batons and the high-pitched tones pierce the air. I howl as the zappers discharge simultaneously. A wall of electricity floods the compound, beams crisscrossing, smashing whatever they touch. The tree shatters high above us, thick limbs falling to the ground and barely missing us. The smell of boiled chlorophyll and burnt wood fills the air. I glance over and see that Junebug and Dr. Pao are shaken but unharmed.

I look back at the Maelstrom soldiers, now advancing through the burned landscape. Whatever their orders were previously, the mission has changed. They are storming the yard like a military formation in a full-frontal assault.

"Come with me!" Dr. Pao shouts, and she motions for us to follow as she and Maddie disappear behind a bank of trees, racing toward the thicket of bushes that leads to the barn behind the house.

I get Junebug and Chance moving, and we follow the doctor into the maze, weaving around corners and ducking under bushes. I hear the Maelstrom soldiers cursing behind us, temporarily confused by the maze-like vegetation.

I think we're home free, when a soldier pops out of the bushes up ahead, directly in front of Chance and Junebug. They stop dead in their tracks, shocked at his sudden appearance.

He looks just as surprised to see two kids in front of him, and he stares at Junebug.

"What the— What are you doing—"

Does the soldier know her?

Junebug rears back and kicks him hard in the groin, cutting off his sentence and doubling him over with a grunt of pain.

I leap forward and slam into him, knocking him into a nearby tree, where he passes out.

Chance is stunned, looking from Junebug to me and back.

"You nailed that dude," Chance says, awestruck.

I want to ask Junebug about what just happened, but I hear the high-pitched whine of the zappers recharging behind us.

"Get down!" I scream, and we dive for the ground as the electrical beams surge over our heads, cutting through the bushes, clearing the way.

Dr. Pao jumps up and races to the barn, flinging open the door.

"Defend!!!" she shouts, and the labradoodles surge out of the barn, howling loudly as they stream into the yard, intent on protecting their mother.

Dr. Pao whirls around. "You have to get out of here. Keep the children safe."

Without an earpiece she can no longer understand my words, but I cock my head, communicating that she should come with us.

"I'm staying to defend my home," she says. "I've been waiting to get some payback against these weasels for a long time."

I howl, urging her to be safe, and she nods her understanding.

"There's a tunnel behind the barn," she says. "You'll find the entrance behind the large boulder. That's your way out."

I call to Chance and Junebug, telling them where to meet me.

In the yard, the labradoodles have made contact with the Maelstrom soldiers. I see dozens of fights occurring at the same time, men and dogs in close combat. The doodles may be cute, but they're agile, and they know how to fight. They use their communication skills to coordinate so two or three doodles pounce on one soldier, incapacitating him before moving on to the next.

They're putting up a good defense, but they're outnumbered, and it's only a matter of time before they're defeated.

"One last thing," Dr. Pao says. "Don't let them take you back to their base, Wild. Do whatever you have to, but don't go back."

"What's back there?" I ask, but the doctor can't understand me, and there's no time for more questions.

She runs into the burning yard behind me, as I head for the back of the barn to find Chance and Junebug.

I dive behind the boulder and find Junebug crouching in fear.

"I lost Chance!" she says. "He went to find you."

She points back toward where I just came from.

I stare at her, wondering if I can trust her after what I thought I saw between her and the soldier.

"What should we do?" Junebug asks frantically.

Her face is etched with worry. I've trusted her this far, and she hasn't let us down.

"I'll find Chance," I say. "You get to the car."

She hesitates, not wanting to separate, but I urge her toward the exit tunnel Dr. Pao told me about.

"Promise you'll protect him," she says.

I lick her face once to reassure her, and she smiles weakly and dives into the tunnel.

Then I turn my full attention to finding Chance.

I race back around the barn, trying to locate Chance's scent, but my nose is overwhelmed by the smoke in the air and the smell of multiple dogs and men.

I catch the barest hint of his scent nearby, and I follow as the trail gets stronger. His normal scent is mixed with sweat and fear, and I speed up, desperate to find him.

I turn the corner lightning fast and hear Chance shout.

"Watch out, Wild!"

A Maelstrom soldier has an arm around Chance's throat, holding him tight. He also has a fully charged zapper with sparks flying from the tip.

It takes only a split second to understand what I'm seeing.

This soldier knew I'd come for Chance, and he waited for me. The moment I appear, the zapper is already rising in his hand, aimed at me, his finger on its trigger.

I see Chance looking at the weapon, struggling, terror in his eyes.

There's no time.

In the space of a breath, the soldier presses the trigger and a beam of electricity arcs from the zapper toward me, sizzling through the air on its lethal course.

As fast as I am, there's no way I can avoid it.

"NOOO!" Chance shouts. He's already in motion as the shot goes off, twisting in the soldier's grip, something glinting in his hand.

It's his cell phone. The only link to his mother.

Chance swings his clenched fist, smashing the phone into the side of the soldier's head. I hear the crunch of the screen breaking and a grunt of pain.

The zapper beam arcs up and away, missing me by a centimeter, singeing the fur on my head and blasting through the tree behind me.

The soldier winces, blood running from a cut near his eye. He loosens his grip around Chance's throat.

This is my opportunity.

I leap into the air, covering the distance between us in a second. I crash into the soldier at full force, knocking him back into a tree where he drops the zapper and crumples, unconscious.

I loom over him, anger like fire in my chest. I want to tear this soldier apart for hurting Chance, rip open his uniform, and—

"Wild!"

Chance calls my name. He's bent over, gasping for breath, hands on his knees. I growl at the soldier one last time, longing for the taste of his blood on my tongue.

Chance's cries bring me back to my senses. I whip around, tail flying, as I forget about the soldier and run to Chance, frantically licking his face to be sure he's okay.

"That tickles," he says, and he laughs and pushes me back.

"You saved my life," I tell him.

"Not really."

"You were incredible, Chance."

He blushes, his cheeks glowing red. But his expression

quickly turns to dismay as he looks down at his cell phone. It's strewn across the ground nearby, screen smashed, case dangling open.

He scoops up the phone in two hands and stares at it for a second.

"Oh well," he says, and he puts the pieces into the backpack on his shoulder.

"You destroyed your phone," I say.

"You're my best friend, Wild. I'd do anything for you."

I see the way he looks at me with love in his eyes, and warmth spreads across my chest and up my back.

"I'd do anything for you, too," I say, the words spilling out, surprising me.

"I'll find some other way to call my mom," he says.

We're interrupted by the sound of a car horn blaring outside the rear walls of the compound. I hear the powerful BMW engine revving and feel relieved, knowing I was right to trust her.

"Junebug's here," I say. "We have to go."

"Let's motivate!" Chance says, and he takes off running toward the barn. I turn back to the soldier passed out on the ground. I sniff at his pocket and smell something made of leather.

I tear it open and pull out a black wallet. Inside is an identification badge of some kind.

ANIMAL CARE AND CONTROL
LOS ANGELES COUNTY
AGOURA DIVISION

More soldiers come around the corner, grabbing for their weapons.

I kick the wallet under a bush and race behind the barn where Chance is waiting. I push him through the tunnel and follow close behind. A second later we emerge outside the compound walls and leap into the BMW. Junebug guns the engine, speeding us away from danger.

JUNEBUG DRIVES FAST THROUGH THE WEST VALLEY.

Chance flips open the laptop and pulls up

a map. I look at it over his shoulder.

"I need some directions fast," Junebug says. "I'm kind of lost up here. The Valley's not my thing."

"It's not anyone's thing," Chance says.

Junebug looks scared for the first time, shaken up by the attack at Dr. Pao's house.

"It's going to be okay," I tell her, and I throw my paws up on the back of her seat and stick my head into the front, flapping my ears around to distract her.

She tries a weak smile, but it's quickly replaced by a frown. "We almost died back there," she says. "They found us even though we got rid of the chip. How did they do it?"

"The doctor thought they were watching the house, maybe assuming I'd go there to talk with her."

"But they saw us. They know who we are now," Junebug says.

"They've always known who we were," Chance says. "They came to the group home."

"They knew who you were," Junebug says. "Not me."

"Why are you so freaked out?" Chance asks. "You had plenty of chances to go, but you kept helping us."

Junebug stares at the road ahead.

"It's a little scarier now," she whispers. "I don't know what they want from us."

"It's not us," I say. "It's me. They want me dead."

"What?" Chance's face goes slack.

Junebug hits the brakes, pulling over to the side of the road.

She spins around in the front seat. "How do you know what they want?"

"It was obvious from the way they stormed the doctor's house, wasn't it? Besides, I heard them say it a few days ago at Chance's group home."

"But it doesn't make sense to kill you," Junebug says.

"Make sense to who?" I ask.

Her eyes dart around as she tries to come up with an answer. I can see that she knows more than she's saying, but I'm not sure what she's hiding.

"I thought they were trying to capture you," Chance says, distraught.

"I'm sorry," I say. "I didn't want to worry you."

"That's why that cop wasn't taking us to the station," Junebug says. "And why those soldiers were firing their zappers all over the yard."

"That's why," I say. "Dr. Pao thinks I'm a Maelstrom dog."

"What does that mean?" Chance asks.

"It means they created me," I say.

"Wild has their secrets inside of her," Junebug says. "And she's proof they exist."

"They don't want anyone to know they exist?" Chance asks.

"Why else would they be disguised as Animal Control officers?" Junebug asks. "And where do they get all that advanced tech they're using?"

"You said they were military," Chance says.

"The military can't operate on US soil," Junebug says.

"How do you know that?"

"I told you, my father's a doomsday prepper." Junebug opens a search window on her laptop. "It's called the Posse Comitatus Act. It's a federal ruling that says military troops can't enforce domestic law."

"So Maelstrom is some kind of secret organization," I say.

"And the secret is out and walking around Los Angeles," Junebug says, pointing to me.

It gets quiet in the car, each of us contemplating the danger we're in.

Chance shivers in the seat next to me. "How do we get you away from them, Wild?"

"Maybe we don't," I say. "Maybe it's time to go our separate ways."

"Absolutely not," Junebug says.

I look up, surprised.

"She's right. We're in this together," Chance says.

I look at Junebug, her jaw set tight. Chance's fists are clenched, and he sits rigid in his seat.

Both of them are determined to fight back.

"All right, then," I say. "We're in it together." The kids start to cheer. "But only for a short time."

"What?" Chance says.

"We stay together and we stay safe, but only until I get Chance back to his mom, and Junebug back to her father."

Junebug grumbles.

"Deal?" I ask.

Chance inhales sharply. "What will you do after?"

I put a paw gently on his arm. "That's not for you to worry about. Now, do we have a deal?"

"Deal," Chance says grudgingly.

"For me, too," Junebug says.

I look over the seat at the map on Junebug's screen.

"Head up the road about half a mile and take a left," I say. "I have an idea where we can go."

WE DRIVE INTO THE MOUNTAINS.

Hidden Hills is on the edge of the mountains

of Malibu Creek State Park. We stop halfway up the mountain road and ditch the car, pushing it into the forest and covering the tracks so it won't be seen from the road. I have the children transfer as much food and equipment as they can carry into the backpacks Ruben loaned us.

"We're really close to Dr. Pao's house," Junebug says.

"That's the point. They'll expect us to run, so we hide nearby in the mountains."

"You're a smart dog," Junebug says.

"Evidently one of the smartest," I say with a laugh.

"But it's scary up here," Chance says. "What if we have to escape fast?"

"Look around," I say. "There's only one road in and out. If they try anything, we'll see them coming from far away."

"I guess," Chance says.

"Hey, we just survived a military attack. Why not do some mountain climbing, too?" Junebug says.

Chance laughs nervously. "Fine, you guys. Whatever. Let's do it."

We begin our hike up the mountain. There's a double peak across the canyon like a sideways letter *K*. I use the landmark to navigate, keeping us moving northwest.

"What do you think happened to Dr. Pao?" Chance asks.

"I don't know exactly. I'm glad she had her dogs to protect her."

"But the soldiers had weapons."

Junebug glances back at me. I can see she's thinking the same thing.

"I'm sure she's all right," I say, even though I can't be certain. I'm worried about her labradoodles, too. They were cute, and they were like a family. It seems that every time I get near anybody, they end up being hurt.

I look up ahead where Junebug is struggling to walk over a loose patch of dirt. Chance reaches out to give her a hand, and they steady each other, finding their way across the rocky ground.

We're becoming like a family, too. What's going to happen to us?

"You're awfully quiet back there," Junebug says to me.

"I'm focused on keeping us safe."

Chance nods. "Safe sounds good to me."

We walk in silence for a long time after that, moving up the mountain until the sun gets low in the sky.

We come to an area near the crest of a small mountain ridge. It's well hidden in a bank of trees, yet it allows a good line of sight around us.

"Let's stop here and camp for the night," I say.

"I don't see a campsite anywhere," Chance says.

"We have to make our own."

"You mean we're sleeping in the forest? There are all kinds of bugs out here. And snakes. And who knows what else," Chance says.

"Are you afraid of bugs?" Junebug asks, rolling her eyes.

"Not afraid. I just don't like them crawling on me while I sleep. And what about a bathroom?"

"Nature is our bathroom."

"Gross." Chance makes a disgusted face.

"I've been camping plenty of times," Junebug says. "You just use the leaves to wipe—"

"I'm starting to change my mind about the benefits of homeschooling," Chance says, waving his hands in surrender.

"My dad likes to rough it, and he has a place in the mountains."

"Big surprise there," Chance says flatly.

"We used to go on vacation a lot. It's like his own secret hideaway. It's near Point Mugu, maybe thirty-five miles from here."

"Point Mugu? If it's close, maybe we could go and ask for his help," Chance says.

"I'm sure he's not around," Junebug says. "He's on a business trip this week, which is why I thought the car thing wouldn't be a problem."

"How did he—"

"He watches me like a hawk. He was probably tracking the car's GPS."

"On second thought, maybe Point Mugu is not a great idea," Chance says.

I want to ask her more about her father, but we have work to do, so I let it pass for the time being.

We set up camp, clearing brush and laying out bedrolls and blankets. Junebug suggests creating a security perimeter with leaves and dried branches so we'll hear any intruders before they get too close.

I tell her it's a good idea. We leave Chance with the supplies, while Junebug and I walk out together to collect materials and scout around the area.

"I was thinking about the first time we spoke," I say.

"You mean when our signals crossed. That was interesting, wasn't it?"

"How did they cross exactly? What were you doing?"

Dr. Pao was right. There's a lot I don't know about Junebug, and it's time I find out more, especially if I'm going to keep her near Chance and me for a few days.

"I was listening to Homeland Security operations around Los Angeles," Junebug says.

"You were hacking Homeland Security?"

"Not hacking. Just listening. I like to listen to radio comms—Homeland Security, the FBI, even regular police frequencies."

She lays down sticks in concentric circles with space between them. If an intruder were to avoid one layer without making a sound, they'd step on the next one and give themselves away.

"That day I heard the Animal Control chatter first. It

didn't sound like anything I'd heard before, and it got my attention. Then I saw your chip transmitting, and I realized you were the one they were talking about."

I watch in amazement as she gathers leaves and uses them to camouflage the perimeter. She's obviously done this before.

"Why do you listen to security communications, Junebug? Is it a hobby of some kind?"

She snaps a branch across her thigh. "My mom was an FBI agent," she says.

"Was?"

"She's dead, Wild. She died on assignment three years ago."

"I'm sorry to hear it."

Her face is calm, but I can sense her pain under the surface.

"My dad got weird after that. He got really strict and he added survival skills to my homeschooling."

She adds dry twigs to the perimeter to amplify the sound if someone steps on them.

"So that's how you learned to make a perimeter like this."

"I learned how to do a lot of things."

She stops and stares at me, frowning. I can feel her irritation—she doesn't like that I'm questioning her.

"I listen to radio comms because they remind me of my dead mom. Okay? Are you satisfied? Interrogation over."

Her face is red and she's breathing heavy, obviously upset.

"It's not an interrogation," I say. "You've been helping us, and I appreciate that, but it's normal that I'd have some questions."

"Maybe I have some questions, too. Like how are you going to keep us safe when we've got a secret military force after us?"

"It's a fair question."

"But you don't have an answer, do you? You act like top dog when you're talking to Chance, but you don't really have a plan." She confronts me, hands on hips as she stares me down.

"I told you. My plan is to stay under the radar until I can get you home."

"And after?"

I lick my paw, stalling for time.

"What about after?" she demands.

"I don't know," I admit. "Once you're safe, I'll figure something out."

"I thought so," she says, and her anger softens. "You know Chance would do anything for you, right? He wants to help you find your home."

"I know."

"I don't think he'll leave you. Even if you ask him to."

I lick my muzzle, fearful that what she's saying is true.

"Make sure you don't ruin his chance to go home. You got that, Wild?"

"Got it. What about you? Aren't you worried about getting home?"

She sighs and drops down cross-legged, staring at the ground in front of her. I trot over and plant myself next to her.

"I lied to that cop yesterday," she says softly. "I really did steal my dad's car. I hate him, and I wanted to get away for a while. I figured he wouldn't care since he was out of town."

"How did he figure it out?"

"Probably our spying neighbor. Or GPS. Or whatever. He's tricky like that."

"Don't you think your dad is worried about you?"

"Not all parents care about their kids, Wild. You're a dog, so everyone wants to pet you and act all nice to you. Maybe you don't know that people are complicated."

I drop my chin on my front paws.

"I am a dog. But I understand more than you think I do."

"Maybe that's true," Junebug says.

I listen to the crickets chirping, their song carried on the wind. It's getting late.

"We should get back before dark," I say.

"For sure."

I stand and kick some leaves into place, finishing off the perimeter. Junebug stretches and breathes in the mountain air.

"You have to go home eventually," I say.

"Eventually I will," she says, turning back toward camp. "Once I'm done helping you."

WE STAY HIDDEN.

There are recreation areas dotted throughout these mountains, but I don't let the kids light a fire. There's no reason to test fate with a smoke trail. It's going to be a cold night, but the blankets Ruben provided should be enough to keep us warm.

I walk around the kids, assessing their health after our long, intense day.

"You're both scratched up from our walk through the woods. There's hydrogen peroxide and gauze in one of the backpacks."

"On it," Junebug says.

She grabs the backpack and brings it over.

"You've got blood on your shirt," she tells Chance. "Take it off so I can clean you up."

"Take off my shirt?"

"Are you embarrassed?"

Chance shivers and looks down. "Of course not. It's just a little cold out."

She rolls her eyes. "Pretend I'm your sister."

He pulls off his shirt, and she dabs at him with the hydrogen peroxide.

I leave them alone and finish setting up the campsite. I pull our bedding into a tight circle, and I walk the area, scanning for any vulnerabilities I might have missed.

"I'll fix your phone tomorrow," I hear Junebug saying. "I can use parts from one of the flashlights if I need to."

"You know how to do everything," Chance says admiringly.

"Not everything."

"A lot more than me. I'm pretty useless at most things, really."

"You're good at taking care of Wild."

I smile inwardly as I think of Chance bringing me home the first night, risking a lot to sneak a stray dog into his room.

"We sort of take care of each other," Chance says.

"I know how to do things because my dad's a fanatic. He forced me to learn all this stuff so I'd be ready for anything."

"At least he cares," Chance says quietly.

"Your dad doesn't care?"

"I don't even know my dad."

"What about your mom?" she asks.

"She has a lot of problems. It makes it hard for her to care as much as she wants to."

I stand in the wind, letting the scents roll up the mountain. I smell pine, earth, and the musty odor of foliage rotting on the forest floor.

I've smelled these things before, I realize.

"My turn to get cleaned up," Junebug says back at camp.

I hear the sound of fabric rustling as she pulls off her shirt.

"Oh my gosh," Chance says.

"What's the big deal? I'm wearing a sports bra. It's just like a bathing suit."

"A bathing suit. Right. What's the big deal?" Chance says, but I hear the nervousness in his voice.

I step out farther from camp, leaping over and around the security perimeter laid out by Junebug. I walk to the highest point nearby and look down the slope.

Something tugs at my memory.

Have I been here before?

I try to remember, but nothing comes.

I turn back toward camp, disappointed, but knowing my job is to get the children home safely before I focus on myself.

The forest is silent around us, which leads me to think we're okay, at least for the night.

And in the morning?

The badge in the soldier's pocket said he was from the Agoura Division of Animal Control. The Animal Control thing is obviously a cover, but if there's a real base in Agoura, it might lead me to Maelstrom.

Once I get the others to safety, that's where I'll begin.

I head back to camp, following the sound of Chance and Junebug's conversation.

I give out a low bark as I get closer to let them know I'm coming.

"It's almost dark," I say. "Let's eat something and go to bed. We'll get an early start tomorrow, then we're heading back into the city to Chance's group home."

"No!" Chance says.

"We'll discuss the details in the morning," I say.

He wants to argue, but Junebug puts an arm around his shoulder. "It'll be okay," she assures him.

We eat quickly, grateful for the food Ruben packed for us. I notice the kids yawning between bites, and I sense their exhaustion from the long day we've had. By the time we're done it's pitch-black in the forest, and I have them under their blankets, a bed of dry pine needles beneath to insulate from the cold ground.

"Good night, you guys."

"You have to sleep, too," Chance says.

I'm as exhausted as they are, but it's not time for me to sleep.

"I'm going to sit up and keep watch," I tell Chance.

He smiles and rubs at his eyes, pulling the blanket up to his neck.

I walk the perimeter one last time, my nose in the wind, scanning for the scent of danger.

"Why do you call yourself Junebug?" I hear Chance whisper. "They're ugly, aren't they?"

"They're super tough," Junebug says. "They fling themselves at the light, and they don't stop until they get where they want to go. I'm like a hacker version of a junebug."

"Do you have a real name?"

There's a pause, and then Junebug says, "Jasmine."

"Good night, Jasmine."

Jasmine. It doesn't ring any bells for me.

"What's your real name?" she asks him.

"You know my real name. Chance."

"How'd you get it?"

"My mom said I was her chance for a new life."

"It's a cool name," Junebug says.

"I think so, too."

Junebug giggles appreciatively, and the conversation ends. Within minutes they're asleep, their breathing slow and heavy. I walk back into the middle of camp where I can watch over them. I feel a powerful protective instinct swelling my chest. This is my pack now, and I will protect my pack at all costs. I briefly think of tomorrow and the separation to come, but it's too painful to imagine, and I have to let it go.

I listen to the sound of crickets chirping in the night air. Eventually my eyes grow heavy, and I drift off to sleep.

THE DREAM RETURNS.

The blond soldier screams as I attack.

The dream is more detailed this time. The soldier holds a black zapper weapon in his hands like the Maelstrom soldiers. I go after the weapon first, clamping down on his wrist and forcing him to drop it.

As soon as it hits the ground, I change direction and attack his midsection.

"Are you okay, Wild?"

Chance's voice is in my ear, pulling me up out of the dream.

I hear myself panting in the night.

The dream is about a Maelstrom soldier. Which means I've fought these people before.

I shiver from snout to tail, shaking the dream away.

A moment later, Chance slides in behind me. He pulls the blanket over us and wraps his arm around me, tucking himself against my back.

I breathe slowly, resisting the instinct to fight or flee.

"Were you having a bad dream again?" Chance asks.

"Again?"

"I've heard you barking in your sleep the last two nights."

We've never been this close. He squeezes me tighter, burying his face in the fur on my back.

"Do you think we're going to be okay?" he whispers.

"I know we are."

"I don't want to go home."

"Why not?"

"I don't want to leave you."

I sigh and settle in, allowing myself to relax in his embrace.

"I have to get you back to your mother," I say. "You need each other."

"That's true," he says. "But I need you, too."

I snuggle closer. His breathing deepens and he falls asleep, snoring lightly in my ear.

I close my eyes and feel Chance's body against mine. My breathing falls into rhythm with his, and I drift back to sleep.

The dream does not come again.

But something else does.

HIS SCENT IS MASKED.

Otherwise I would have smelled this creature, even in my sleep. But somehow his scent is hidden, so he is inside the camp before I know it. He's almost on top of us when the crunch of sycamore leaves gives him away.

My eyes snap open and I instantly leap up, guarding the children in a protective posture.

"What's going on?" Chance mutters, half-asleep.

"I'm not s—"

The creature springs before I've even finished my sentence, leaping out of the darkness and crashing into me with such force that the air rushes from my lungs and I'm sent sprawling. He hits me hard again and we roll over and over through the brush.

He leaps away from me, and I stand quickly, my head spinning as I get my balance. I look behind me and gasp.

I'm on the edge of a cliff, the earth dropping away into nothing a few inches from my paws. I regain my footing and move away from the edge.

"Watch yourself. It's a long way down," the dog says.

"Where are you?!" I demand, snorting and trying to draw the creature into the open.

I edge forward, marking the location of the mountain cliff behind me.

The wind shifts, and the smell hits me.

The creature's scent has been masked beneath a chemical layer, but once the layer is disturbed, the smell is *unmistakable*.

Male dog.

Not just any dog, but something abnormal, savage, bordering on feral.

Chance shouts, "Where are you, Wild?"

He's still back at camp looking for me, and the dog's head whips around, tracking the sound of his voice.

I snarl, pulling the dog's attention back to me.

His eyes glow ghostly red in the moonlight. I look around, scanning the area for additional dogs or men.

"There's no one else," he hisses. "Only me."

I'm startled by his ability to speak. His voice is low and empty like wind echoing through a canyon.

"You can talk like the humans," I say.

"Of course I can. *We* can. Why does that surprise you?"

"I didn't know there was anyone else like me," I say.

"But we've spoken many times before."

"I don't know who you are," I admit.

He barks laughter. "You lost your memory. They didn't tell me about that."

"Did they tell you I was zapped in the head and left for dead?"

"Ugly business," he says.

The moon peeks out of the clouds above us, and I catch a glimpse of him. He's much larger than me, and he stands on huge paws. His furry tail whips through the air.

"I had nothing to do with you being zapped," he says. "But I give you credit. You're one tough dog to be able to survive that. Which makes what's about to happen a great shame."

"What do you mean?" I ask.

"You survived being zapped, but you're not going to survive this night."

He leaps, jaws open, fangs bared.

I avoid his mouth, jumping to my front paws, then kicking out with my rear, a move that's worked for me before.

I connect with his side, but it's like kicking a stone wall. His muscles are thick beneath his skin, and unlike previous times, my kick barely registers.

Flashlights snap on in the campsite behind us, and I hear Chance and Junebug's shouts as they search for me. They're too far away for me to warn them, and I don't want to bark and risk bringing them closer.

"You must have expected we'd come for you," he says.

"I knew the blue uniforms were after me. I didn't know there were dogs, too."

"I've been tracking you since before Dr. Pao's."

"How is that possible?"

"I'm thirty-seven percent bloodhound. A super sniffer, among other things."

I hear the sound of Chance and Junebug's footsteps moving through the forest.

"Then the soldiers will be here soon," I say.

"I work independently," he says. "They do it their way, I do it mine. You don't remember how it works with us."

I'm afraid of this dog, but hungry for the information he knows.

"Tell me how it works," I ask him.

"Every dog has a specialty. Mine is tying up loose ends. That's why they call me the Finisher."

"The Finisher."

"It's why I'm here. Unfinished business."

"What's my specialty?"

He sneers, his breath forming a cloud in the frigid air. "You make people love you."

"But why?"

"Because you have a job to do," he says. "You're one of us, a Maelstrom dog."

I yelp in distress as my suspicion is confirmed.

"Big girls don't cry," he sneers.

I clamp the sound in my throat, ashamed to be caught in a vulnerable moment in front of this animal.

"You're one of us. You must have figured that out by now."

I back up, my body instinctively trying to get away from his words. I'm hyperaware of the cliff's edge behind me, and I shuffle to the side, being careful to avoid it.

As I move, I feel the unevenness of the forest floor beneath me, and something clicks in my head.

Gain the advantage.

If I can get to higher ground, I'll have a slight advantage in an attack.

"If I am a Maelstrom dog," I say, "why are they after me?"

"You went rogue," he says simply.

"What does that mean?"

I shift to my left, moving up a slight incline as I try to keep him talking.

"I know what you're doing," he says. "It's what I would do in your situation."

He attacks instantly, staying low and coming for my belly, trying to use my position against me. I sense his moves before he makes them, and I crouch, avoiding his teeth and delivering a fast, defensive nip to his hindquarters.

He yelps and jerks away, backing up a few steps to reorient himself.

"Just a scratch," he says.

His blood-soaked fur tastes disgusting, and I feel my stomach churn. I remember the taste of Thunder in my mouth and the way it made me feel.

He walks into the moonlight, revealing himself for the first time. He's an awkward mix of breeds, big and thick-haired like a Siberian husky, yet with the shortened snout of a bloodhound and big jowls.

He howls into the air, a high, warbling note like a demented laugh.

"You think you're better than me," he says.

"I don't even remember you."

"But I can feel your disdain. It was there before, and it's still here now. You think you're special, that you don't have to follow orders, and that makes you better than me. But the truth is we're the same."

"We're not the same. You're a killer—all you know is fighting."

"We're both killers. You're just sneaky about it."

He leaps forward, snarling.

"I don't want to fight you," I say.

"You have no choice, my friend."

"I'm not your friend."

"You used to be." He charges like a wild animal, teeth bared.

I do my best to avoid the attack. I slam at him with my paws, then I throw warning nips, then I pivot and try to get away. But nothing seems to put him off.

He connects with a bite to my midsection. I hear his teeth crunch down, and I howl and twist, forcing him to release me.

But the damage is done. I feel blood flowing freely from a wound underneath me.

He backs up, rage in his eyes.

"I can see why they wanted to keep you," he says. "You're talented. Even when you started to rebel, they tried to work with you, at least until you snapped and gave them no choice but to destroy you."

Flashlight beams bounce off the trees nearby.

"Wild!" Chance shouts.

He's found me, and he's only a few feet away, unaware of the danger he's in.

The dog turns to Chance, his eyes red, drool flowing. He charges without warning, aiming directly for the flashlight beam in Chance's hand.

I howl and attack, my heart pumping, eyes blind with rage. I crash into him from the side, catching him off guard, and my jaws close around his neck.

Chance screams, surprised by the chaos in the dark in front of him.

"What's happening?!" Junebug shouts.

The Maelstrom dog squirms, his throat vulnerable between my teeth. I hold him by the neck, not biting but not releasing, controlling him with the tension in my jaws.

He thrashes, and his sharp nails scratch my side. He whines and tries to turn his head to bite. I don't know how long I can hold him like this.

Chance's flashlight finds me in the forest, and he gasps as he sees me with this dog. I know I'm covered in blood and wounded, and I can only imagine what I look like with this dog in my mouth.

"What are you doing, Wild? Who is that dog?"

I can't answer, can't speak with my mouth full of this animal, the terrible smell of him in my nose.

"What's going on?!"

It's Junebug, racing out of the forest to find Chance staring at us. Her flashlight beam joins his, lighting me up as if I'm onstage.

The Maelstrom dog's eyes are wide, and he thrashes

again. At first I think he's trying to get away, and then I realize what he really wants.

He's trying to get to the children.

He jerks in their direction, jaws snapping, fighting to get away from me so he can get to them.

I don't care about the foul taste of him in my mouth, or the flashlight beams dancing across us, or Chance shouting for Junebug to hurry. I can't let the Finisher hurt the kids.

I crouch, muscles rippling in my legs, and I twist and throw him high into the air, as hard and as far as I can.

He lands at the cliff's edge, scrambling to gain purchase on the loose gravel. His eyes go wide with fear.

I realize what's happening, and I'm torn between saving him or letting him fall.

We are the same, I hear him say, but I don't know if he's said it again or I'm remembering it from earlier.

"We're not the same," I shout, rushing forward to help him.

But I'm too late. The Finisher loses his balance and goes over the cliff, howling as he falls.

I make it to the edge a second later and look down. I search the dark landscape for evidence of the Finisher. Did he land? Did he die? It's impossible to tell.

"What did you do?" Chance asks.

The flashlights hit my eyes, causing me to blink.

"Did you hurt that dog?" Junebug asks.

"I didn't— It was him or us."

Chance and Junebug stare at me, confused by the fight

they've seen. The look of horror on their faces is too much for me, and I turn away in shame.

I can still taste the Finisher's blood on my muzzle. I take a step toward Chance, and he backs up.

"You killed him," Chance says, horror on his face.

"I tried to save him. He attacked our camp, and I had to—"

I start to explain, but my words sound hollow, and Chance's eyes are filled with fear.

"They'll be coming for us soon," I say. "Head back to camp and get ready to leave. I'll be right behind you."

The kids stumble away, flashlight beams swinging in front of them. When they're out of earshot, I run to the cliff and take a final look into the inky blackness. I scan the ground below, but there's nothing down there.

No body, no dog, no tracks of any kind.

THE SKY GLOWS OVER THE TREE LINE.

I clean myself in the river, washing out my wounds. The dog bite is bad, but not fatal, and the cold river water takes some of the pain away. What it can't take away is the smell of the Finisher. When I step out of the water, his scent is still on me and the taste of his fur lingers in my mouth.

It was kill or be killed.

That's what I tell myself, but it's not the whole truth.

Something in me enjoyed hurting the Maelstrom dog. It felt like revenge, and it felt good.

Maybe he was right, and we're both killers. I can't be sure.

I smell Chance's scent on the wind, and it pulls me back to the moment. I shiver in the cool dawn air, shaking off water from head to tail. Then I hurry back toward camp to check on the children.

Chance and Junebug have packed up in my absence,

and they're waiting with their backpacks by their sides.

Junebug is startled to see me, and she backs up a little when I come out of the woods.

Is she afraid of me?

I drop my head and whimper, reacting instinctively to the disapproval I feel.

Chance turns when he hears me, his face a mask of concern. "Are you hurt?"

I check the dog bite and realize it's already stopped bleeding. My metabolism is revving high, speeding up the healing process.

"I'll be fine," I say. "What about you two?"

"We're okay," Junebug says, but I can feel the tension in the air, and I notice she stays back, maintaining some distance from me.

"We should get out of here," Junebug says. "The soldiers will be coming for us."

"We have a little time," I say. "That dog worked alone as a hunter."

"He was hunting you?" Chance says anxiously.

I nod. "Turns out there are soldiers *and* dogs after me."

"Then we need to go," Chance says.

I lick my lips and the taste of the Finisher makes my stomach churn.

I hear Dr. Pao's voice in my head:

You're not a pet, Wild. You're a weaponized animal, bred for intelligence, bred for strength and violence.

I turn away from the kids. "I have to leave for a while."

Chance steps back as if hit by an invisible blow.

"What— Where will you go?"

"I need some time alone to think about our next move."

"We know our next move. We're going home," Chance says.

It's hard to hear him so upset, and I fight my desire to stay and soothe him. The truth is I don't trust myself anymore, and I'm afraid of what might happen if I stay near him.

"The best strategy is to separate," I say.

"Really?" Junebug stares at me, hands on her hips.

I look up to meet her eye. "If there are other Maelstrom dogs nearby, they'll follow my trail and I'll lead them away from you."

"You mean there might be more of those things?" Chance asks, his arm shaking as he points back to the scene of the fight.

"It's possible," I say.

"And you want us to get home without you?" Junebug says. "How does that make sense?"

"You'll follow the same path down the mountain, and I'll catch up to you when I'm sure it's safe."

"When will that be?" Chance asks. He looks scared and small, standing there in the half-light.

I don't have an answer for him, and it's too painful to lie.

"The sun's coming up. You'd better get going."

Chance takes a step toward me, and Junebug puts an arm out to stop him. He pushes through her arm and rushes toward me, dropping to his knees, his face even with my own.

He leans in and looks me in the eye.

"Take care of yourself, Wild. When we get down, we'll head for the group home. I'll see you there, if not before."

I turn away, unwilling to tell him the truth—that I don't think we'll ever see each other again.

I RUN.

Through the forest, up and down embankments, fighting my way through thick undergrowth only to run some more.

I don't know where I'm going, but I know what my direction must be.

Away.

I want to get as far away from the children as I can. Or maybe it's the truth I'm running from.

Dr. Pao warned me that I had the instincts of a killer built into my genetic code.

I didn't want to believe her.

But I felt the instinct come alive during the fight with the Finisher, and now I know she was telling the truth. Maybe I've known it all along. The dreams were telling me what I'd done, but I didn't want to listen.

Maybe you'd be better off not knowing what's out there, Ruben said.

I wanted to know, and now I do.

I'm a violent dog, created by Maelstrom. They've made me what I am and taken away my chance of finding a home.

I don't belong with dogs, but how can I live with humans? A feeling of despair and pain washes through me.

Now they're after me, and they won't stop. Dogs, soldiers, whatever else they might have at their disposal. I think about a future of running and fighting, and my body is overcome with exhaustion.

I slow to a trot, looking for someplace where I can lie down for a while. A hiding place that will give me time to rest and to heal.

I spot an outcropping nearby with a narrow cave opening beneath it. I crawl into the cave on failing legs, squeezing through the crack in the rocks and into the fetid black hole. My body is shutting down, forcing me to rest so it can heal.

I lie in the dark listening to the sound of my chest heaving. I feel the blood dripping from my wound and taste the dog's stinking fur in my muzzle.

Occasionally I think of the kids, but I push the image from my mind. Instead I look into the darkness, choosing the dark and the cold as my companions.

I slip in and out of consciousness.

Maybe I sleep. I can't be sure.

Gradually I become aware of a noise. A low hum, vibrating through the stones above me.

I can't tell if I'm awake or dreaming. And then the hum gets louder, the pitch rising and fading as it moves away.

There's something familiar about that sound.

A helicopter.

I crawl my way out of the cave, moving from pitch-black to inky night.

It's dark now. *Did I sleep through the day?*

I hear the noise again, the unmistakable sound of helicopter blades chopping through the air. If one already went by, this must be a second one.

A minute later a helicopter skims the tree line above me, heading away at speed.

I catch a glimpse of it between the branches. It's a twin-engine Black Hawk, a military helicopter, flying low and carrying a heavy load. I see blue uniforms through the windows on the cargo door.

Maelstrom soldiers. *Where are they coming from?*

I orient myself with the moon, quickly getting my bearings on the mountain range. The helicopters are heading north, and I look south, scanning for familiar features.

That's when I see the double peak like a letter к on its side. I look across the canyon to where our campsite was located. It's nearly ten miles away, but I can see that the tops of the trees are disturbed near the area where we'd set up camp. The leaves have been blown right off by the blast of the rotors.

The helicopters were at the campsite.

I start to run.

THE SITE HAS BEEN DESTROYED.

Dozens of bootprints mark the area where the soldiers tracked through camp looking for us. I follow the prints down the mountain, my heart pounding as I trace the path that Chance and Junebug took as they fled from the soldiers. I race along for several miles before I see the broken branches and trampled foliage that are evidence of a fight. The kids' backpacks are torn open and flung aside.

This is where the soldiers caught up to them. I can still smell the uniforms combined with the fuel of the Black Hawk helicopter that carried them here.

I call out to Chance and Junebug, howling into the forest, but nothing comes back except the echo of my own voice.

The scents on the forest floor tell the story. The children ran until the soldiers caught them. They struggled as best they could, but they were overpowered and carried away, at which point their scents disappear entirely.

I whine with frustration and rage that I wasn't here to protect them when they needed me.

A flash of light catches my eye. I see a glint of metal on the ground behind a tree and run toward it.

It's Junebug's laptop. It's tucked between the tree roots and half-covered with leaves. Junebug would never leave her laptop unless . . .

She hid it here on purpose, hoping I would come back and find it.

I scrape off the leaves and nudge it open with the tip of my nose.

Junebug has turned off her security, and the screen lights up as soon as I touch a key.

I'm looking at a Google map of the California coast. There's a location pinned forty miles north of here, in the direction the helicopters were flying.

It's a different mountain range than the one I'm standing on. I study the area around it, a deserted expanse far from cities and developments. I look for anything I might recognize, any clue at all.

That's when I see it.

Point Mugu.

That's where they've taken the kids, so that's where I'll go.

THE SMELL OF FUEL HANGS HEAVY IN THE AIR.

Without the smell, it would be all but impossible to find this base, buried as it is within a valley in Point Mugu State Park, completely hidden from view, with only a single road leading in and out.

I stand out of sight and study it from above. My ears tingle, and I'm hit by a flash of memory.

I'm in a sterile white laboratory, strapped to a table as dogs stare down at me from above. The memory is like ice on my paws.

This base. I've been here before.

It's much smaller than I expected, a half-mile-wide clearing in the mountains surrounded by a high electrified fence topped with razor wire. At first glance it might not be a base at all, perhaps just a remote landing area for Black Hawk helicopters. But the memory suggests there's more here than meets the eye.

The problem is there's nothing much in front of me. No

dog-training center, no holding cells, no place for soldiers to live. I only see a landing strip, a fuel depot, and some kind of low concrete building in the center.

Maybe my memory is playing tricks on me?

I breathe deeply and can smell the barest trace of the children, no more than a few scent molecules lingering in the air, but it's enough for my ultrasensitive nose to detect. Chance and Junebug were here not too long ago.

I smell something else, too. The Maelstrom soldiers. They are somewhere nearby, which means I was right. There's a base here. I sense the truth about where I come from is here, too.

I step forward, and I feel a subtle vibration under my feet. I place my ear to the dirt and listen. I can hear the buzz of machinery and whir of ventilation units far below.

The Maelstrom base is beneath me, buried underground.

I snort and walk in a circle, excited energy building in my body. I have to get inside. The kids are down there, and the clues that will unlock my past as well.

I walk the perimeter, staying out of sight in the forest, looking for any weakness in the defenses.

But the fence is continuous, and there are motion detectors and antipersonnel mines dotting the area. The hum of electricity runs through the fence, a clear warning that one touch is death.

I whine, frustrated, as I work my way back around to the front of the base. An imposing front gate is locked tight and framed with windowless black guard shacks.

There's no way I can get inside.

I stand in the tree line, scratching at the dirt with my rear paws, feeling angry and trapped.

Without warning, a dozen blue-uniformed soldiers surge out of the guard shacks, lining up inside the gate.

Did I somehow trigger an alarm?

A moment later a motor roars to life, and the massive gate in front of the base starts to move.

I PREPARE FOR
A FIGHT.

The gate opens slowly, and I scan the dozen or so soldiers on the other side, men and women, their faces determined as they prepare to defend the base. I decide I will wait for them to come at me, lure them out of the base before I attack. If I can separate and confuse them in the forest, I might be able to take them down one by one.

The gate is all the way open now, but for some reason, the soldiers don't move. They stand, weapons in hand, waiting.

I step out of the tree line, revealing myself to them, daring them to come after me.

They look at me with a mix of fear and awe, but they do not come toward me. The commander raises her hand and gives an order, and the soldiers retract their zappers and place the black batons in their holsters. The line of men and women splits down the middle, opening a path onto the base.

I'm ready to run, when the commander says, "Please come in."

I recognize the voice. She's the same one who shouted commands to us in the PetStar parking lot before Junebug saved us.

I hesitate, sniffing and catching her scent on the wind. It's strong and steady, without the smell of fear I'd expect if someone were setting a trap.

"I know you can understand me," she says. "No one will harm you."

My ears perk up with astonishment.

How does she know I can understand?

I walk through the gate onto the base, sniffing the air for what lies ahead, my senses on high alert. I walk through the gauntlet of soldiers, stopping halfway down the line.

I'm staring at the large Animal Control officer who tried to kill me back at Chance's group home. He looks at me with recognition in his eyes.

I snarl at him, considering my next move.

He stands at attention, watching me under heavy lids. I see a single bead of sweat drip from his brow.

"I remember you," I growl.

He looks at me, uncomprehending. He knows I'm talking to him, but he doesn't know what I'm saying.

The commander clears her throat, drawing my attention forward. She points to the cement building in the center of the base.

"The base is under us," she says. "That's the entrance."

I give the large Animal Control officer one more glance, and then I walk toward the slab of concrete, torn between my curiosity and my desire for revenge.

A lock turns, and a large steel door opens. I walk forward and the main gate of the base grinds shut behind me.

I trot into the building and see an elevator ahead, its doors open, the interior wide enough for two dozen people, yet it's completely empty.

I step inside, and the elevator descends rapidly, dropping deep into the ground beneath the mountain. It takes a full minute before the journey ends, a tone sounds, and the doors open.

I'm standing in a massive underground lab, and I have to steady myself as the familiar sights and smells assault me.

It feels like I've been here hundreds of times before, yet I don't remember where I am or what the purpose of this place is.

It's time to find out.

The entry hall is deserted, but the smell of dogs and humans fills the air. I notice flashes of light coming from a large conference room down the hall. The conference room wall is covered with video monitors, the same scene playing on each one.

The screens show footage from my fight in the forest last night. It seems to have been recorded through a night-vision camera, perhaps positioned on a drone. The Finisher and I move through a ghostly green landscape, our eyes bright spots. We fight savagely, rolling over and over through the brush, attacking, withdrawing, and attacking again.

I hear a noise behind me and whirl around. A man comes through the door. He's wearing a crisply ironed black uniform, a different style than the other Maelstrom soldiers, with none of the fake Animal Control insignia. His lapels are marked with the gold stars of a general. He has closely cropped gray hair and a dark complexion with light green eyes.

"Nice to see you again," he says.

Do I know this man?

He walks past, seemingly unconcerned by my presence as he opens a laptop and taps at a few keys.

I growl to warn him, and he glances up and smiles. "I wouldn't do anything quite yet. You're going to want to see this."

The video footage changes on the screens.

A dog is running through an obstacle course, fighting through muck and leaping over wooden barriers. I see her in different environments, swimming a rushing river, climbing a mountain, crawling through deep sand. I see her dodging weapons fire, attacking humanoid figures by striking at different places on their silicone bodies.

"Look familiar?" he asks.

The dog in the video has the same-colored coat as me. I watch her move through the training exercises, learning the kinds of skills I've used over the last few days.

I grunt in astonishment as the memories gain form.

I was born here.

I look at the young dog on screen jump on her front paws and pivot, kicking out with her rear legs.

"You must recognize yourself in the videos," the man says.

"The older dog and the puppy. They're both me."

"Of course they are. These are like home movies for you. You don't remember living here?"

"Hang on—you can understand me?"

"Every word," he says.

He points to his ear. He's wearing a black earbud, identical to the one from my collar box except for the color.

"How did you get that earbud?" I ask.

He laughs. "The real question is how did *you* get the earbud. And the collar. And everything else that makes you special."

"I don't know what—"

"You got them from me," he says.

I swallow hard and taste fear in the back of my throat.

"Where are Chance and Junebug?" I ask.

He waves away the question like it's unimportant. "I'm the one setting the agenda today."

I get ready to spring, a growl rolling up from my chest.

"Before you do anything stupid, I suggest you look down," he says.

I stare at the shiny black floor beneath my paws. Thin wires are running beneath me, and I can feel the hint of a powerful current causing my paw pads to tingle.

"The floor is electrified," the man says. "The circuit is completed by your collar box."

He opens his hand, revealing a small device with a red button.

"If I press this button while you're anywhere in the facility, you'll be electrified instantly. There's no stun setting and no warning."

I crouch, muscles at the ready, judging the distance from him to me and the time it will take for me to travel that distance.

"I'm fast," I say.

"Not faster than electricity."

"I might be able to get to you before you even press the button."

"You might. But if you kill me, you'll never find out who you really are. Isn't that what you want most?"

I stop growling and back up a step.

He smiles. "I thought so."

He presses the laptop keyboard, and the video screens go black. "I'm a little saddened by your performance today. You were cunning before all of this happened. You would never have walked in here and made yourself vulnerable."

"Is that why you opened the gate? You wanted to see what I would do?"

"I wanted to find out how much you remembered. Besides, we have unfinished business."

I pad across the room, and I see his arm stiffen, the red button tight in his fist.

"Tell me what you did with the children," I say.

"Kids are like an obsession with you, aren't they? You're worried about all the wrong things. I thought we had trained you better."

"Trained me?"

"I'm General Rupani," the man says. "I'm the head of Maelstrom. And this is your home."

Rupani. The general Dr. Pao mentioned.

I sit back, my head spinning, the memories coming in waves.

The general watches me, the device ever present in his hand.

"The kids call you Wild, but we refer to you as She-Nine."

"*She-Nine?*"

"You're the ninth in a series. There have been several iterations of Maelstrom dogs."

"The dog you sent after me in the mountains. He called himself the Finisher."

"Ah yes. He has a flair for the dramatic, doesn't he? We call him He-Seven."

"Seven and nine. You give us numbers?"

"The numbers are the different iterations. He's a hunter. We have others who are experts at hiding, still others with great intelligence."

"And what am I?"

He grins and takes a deep breath. "Ah, the eternal question. What am I, and why am I here?"

"You must know the answer."

"You, my dear, were supposed to be a little bit of everything. The best of the best."

Blood rushes to my head and I stumble, dizzy from the revelation.

"So it's true. You're using CRISPR technology to edit dog genes."

His eyes widen in surprise. "Did Dr. Pao tell you that?"

"That and more. She told me how you stole her company."

He sighs. "Her version of events. Very one-sided. From

my perspective, I saved her company. She only wanted to make pets, but I saw the true possibilities."

"To make a superbreed."

"Sadly, I've made a lot of mistakes along the way. Like you for instance."

"Is that why you tried to kill me?"

"You went rogue, She-Nine. What did you expect me to do?"

Rogue. There's the word again, the same one the Maelstrom dog used to describe me.

Before I can ask the general what he means, I catch wind of Chance and Junebug's scents pushed through the room by the air circulation system, and I feel desperation tighten my chest.

I have to save the kids.

"I know the children are here," I say.

"You can smell them even on the filtered air?"

I nod.

"Impressive." He pulls a pad from his pocket and jots down a quick note.

"I want to see them. Now."

"Your survival is at stake, yet you're worried about those kids. Explain that to me."

"They're my friends," I say.

The general shakes his head. "You weren't designed to have friends or to be reliant on human companionship at all. You make them love you, while you feel nothing."

"Nothing?"

I remember the feeling of Chance lying behind me last

ALLEN ZADOFF

night, his body warm against my back as he slept with his arms wrapped around me. The memory creates a sensation of longing in my chest. I want to be next to him again, right now.

I look at the general. "Maybe you don't know as much about me as you think you do."

We're interrupted by a firm knock at the door.

"Come!" he shouts.

The door opens, and Junebug walks in. I rear back on my hind paws, stunned. She glances at me, then looks away.

"Hi, Daddy," she says, smiling at the general.

I see the resemblance immediately. The general has a dark complexion and light green eyes.

Junebug's eyes.

I snarl as she walks past, but she ignores me and gives the general a hug. He kisses the top of her head, casually draping an arm across her shoulder.

"You've met my daughter, Jasmine," the general says. "She was kind enough to let us know where she was in the mountains so we could come and pick her up. And your little friend Chance, too."

Dr. Pao warned me about Junebug, and she was right. It seems obvious now. The incredible coincidence that brought Junebug into our lives. The reason she had an earbud that could pick up my signal. Her stories of her stern father and the homeschooling and survival lessons.

Junebug is Jasmine Rupani, the general's daughter.

And I missed it.

"I call Jasmine my first and most successful experiment," General Rupani says.

Junebug's face twitches and anger flares around her eyes. A second later it's gone, and she's smiling at her father.

"You were a spy?" I ask coldly.

"It's complicated," she says quietly.

"My daughter got confused and thought she was helping you," the general says. "But then she came to her senses and remembered who she was—and where her loyalties lie."

"You called the soldiers," I say.

"What was I supposed to do?" she says angrily. "You hurt that dog, and then you ran away and left us. You broke your promise to Chance."

The truth stings, and I look away, ashamed to meet her eyes.

"You're dangerous, Wild. I didn't want to believe it—"

"But it's true," the general says to her. "Just like I told you all along."

Junebug stares at me, her eyes tight with anger. "You left Chance alone on a mountain," she says. "I made sure he got out of there safely."

"So you took him home to his mother?"

Junebug frowns and looks to her father. "Not exactly home," she whispers.

The general steps between us. "I have the boy. He'll be our guest for a little while until we straighten out some things."

"Take me to him," I say as I move toward them menacingly.

General Rupani holds up the red button, warning me back.

"We have some business to attend to before you can see him," General Rupani says. "You started a mission six months ago, She-Nine, and you walked away before it was done."

You went rogue, the dog in the forest said to me. Is this what he meant?

"What mission are you talking about?" Despite my anger, I'm curious.

"You were living with a family when—" Junebug hesitates, looking for the right word. "When this all began."

"That's past," the general says with a wave of his hand. "But Jasmine has a brilliant idea for the present. An experiment of sorts."

"A second chance," Junebug says.

She looks at me intently, pleading with her eyes.

What does she want from me?

"I'm not following," I say.

"Instead of killing you," the general says, "we're going to give you a chance to finish the original mission."

My eyesight blurs, the rage and frustration more than I can take. I watch the two of them, furious at the situation I've gotten myself into, the word games, Junebug's deception.

"Why would I work for you?" I ask.

"You'll perform one mission in exchange for Chance's life," he says.

"Dad—" Junebug starts to say, but the general cuts off her protest.

"This is how it has to be," he says quietly.

There's obviously some conflict between them that I can't

understand. For now it doesn't matter. All that matters is Chance's safety.

"One mission?" I ask.

The general walks toward me, the button held by his side. Junebug bites at her thumbnail.

"One mission, She-Nine. You follow my orders. You do what I tell you to do. That's the price."

I think of Chance, alone and afraid, a prisoner somewhere in this facility. If it wasn't for me, he would be safe at the group home now, hours away from being reunited with his mother. Now he's in danger, and it's all my fault.

I'll do anything to keep him safe, even work for this monster.

"I need to know he's okay, or I won't agree to anything."

"Fair enough," the general says with a grin.

THEY BRING ME
TO CHANCE.

He lies on a bed in a small white holding
cell. The front wall is made of clear, hard polymer with a
talk port in the center. The moment he sees me, he runs to
the port and throws himself against it.

My throat tightens when I see how afraid he is. I shake
my head, struggling not to cry out.

"We waited for you as long as we could, then we started
to hike out and they came for us."

"I heard all about it," I say.

"I tried to fight them off, but there were too many of
them. They grabbed Junebug and me."

"You were very brave. I'm sure you did your best."

I see the earbud in his ear. Rupani must have let him keep
it so we could speak.

"Did you come to get me out of here?" Chance asks.

I swallow hard. "Soon."

"But not now."

I shake my head, and his face droops with disappointment. He glances behind me at the Maelstrom soldiers who stand guard at the end of the hall.

"Are you a prisoner, too?" he asks.

"I'm afraid so."

"What about Junebug? They separated us, and I'm worried about her."

I debate whether to tell him the truth but decide it's not the time or place for it. I need him to stay positive and not lose hope.

"I've seen her," I say. "She's okay."

"They captured us and put us on separate helicopters. They asked me a lot of questions about you, but I wouldn't tell them anything. You believe me, right?"

"Of course I believe you. It's not your fault, Chance. None of this is your fault."

"Who are these people?"

"Dr. Pao was right. Animal Control is the cover for Maelstrom. We're inside their base."

"How do we get out? What do they want from us?"

"Not us. Me."

He stares, curious, but I perk up my ears and point my muzzle around the room.

They're listening, Chance.

He blinks, signaling his understanding.

"For now I need you to take care of yourself and trust me."

"Tomorrow," he whispers. "That's the day my mom gets out of treatment. I'm not going to see her again, am I?"

He sniffles, holding back tears. It rips me up inside to see him like that. I want to yelp and lick his face, but I can't get to him through the dividing wall.

"I'm going to get you out of here," I say. "I promise."

Chance puts his palm on the clear wall, and I press my head against it, right where his hand is. I can't feel him petting me, but I know that's what he's trying to do, and it fills me with joy.

We were both alone when we met, but now we've got each other. He's my boy, and I'm his dog.

"Be careful, Wild."

"You, too." He does his best to smile.

The guard whistles to signal our time is up.

I look at Chance for a long moment, memorizing every detail of his face and smelling his familiar scent through the holes in the talk port.

The guard grunts, and I reluctantly turn away from Chance and head for the door.

General Rupani is waiting for me in the hall outside.

"Did you have a nice visit?" he asks.

I growl at him, barely suppressing my rage.

"Tell me what you want me to do," I say.

I CAN SMELL THE OCEAN THROUGH THE CLOSED WINDOWS OF THE VAN.

I'm in the back of a Maelstrom vehicle that's disguised as an Animal Control van. We're driving up the Pacific Coast Highway through Malibu. The large officer who came to Chance's group home is sitting across from me. He tried to kill me a few days ago, but now he and these other men are my partners in a secret operation for Maelstrom. There are other blue-uniformed soldiers in the vehicle as well, but I don't recognize them.

General Rupani explained the situation during a briefing back at the base. He said that six months ago I was placed with the family of the heiress who owns the yacht I woke up on. I was their family pet, or at least I pretended to be, while my real purpose was to spy on them and report back to Maelstrom. Instead of a fly on the wall, I was the dog in the living room, listening to every phone conversation, reading every piece of mail, watching as Helen Horvath typed passwords into her computer. When she traveled, I traveled with her, and the spying continued.

"We need you to go back into the Horvath house," General Rupani said. "We want you to retrieve a computer jump drive."

"Why me?" I asked.

"Helen Horvath keeps it on a chain around her neck, and she never takes it off. We believe it has the access codes to a secret financial network that's being used to fund terrorist activities around the globe. You can get close enough to take it away from her without her realizing immediately."

"A necklace with a jump drive. That's the entire mission? Why would I run away from a mission like that?"

"Some things are better left in the past," General Rupani said. "Your memory loss may turn out to be a blessing. Let's get you back inside that house, and let's focus on the future together."

I wrinkled my nose, disturbed by what I was hearing. "What future are you talking about?"

"Maelstrom was your home, She-Nine. There's no reason it can't be your home again."

Home.

The thing I'd been seeking from the moment I awoke on the yacht. The general was offering me a way back.

But did I want to return to the people who tried to kill me? Could I ever really trust them?

I didn't respond to the general, afraid to say something that might risk Chance's life.

The briefing ended with a simple promise by the general: If I follow orders, he'll release Chance. If I deviate, the agreement is off, and no one will ever see Chance alive again.

Back in the van, the large officer snaps his fingers to get my attention.

"Stay sharp," he says. "We'll be there in one minute."

"Got it," I say, snorting at the smell of this man who I hate.

"We're setting up the command center a mile away down the beach," the officer says. "We'll be monitoring your vital signs through your collar. General Rupani is your handler for this mission. He'll be in constant contact with you."

I bark, letting him know I understand.

"By the way, no hard feelings about the other day, when we shot at you with the zapper," he says. "Lucky we missed, huh?"

He smiles as if we're friends, and I swallow the anger that would have me lash out at him now.

"I was just following orders," he says. "We're soldiers. That's what soldiers do."

Is that what we do? We follow orders even if it means killing one another?

I turn away, unable to deal with this now, and focus my thoughts on the task ahead.

The van pulls off the highway and slows behind a bank of trees. A soldier opens the door to let me out.

"Your destination is about a mile down the road," the large officer says.

I yelp my understanding and hop out of the van, grateful to be away from these people.

I take a deep breath of ocean air and trot down the embankment, darting across the Pacific Coast Highway during a break in the traffic.

I jog along the side of the highway for a while, allowing my fur to pick up dirt and leaves from the underbrush. A few cars slow so their drivers can look at me, probably wondering what a dog is doing running free on the side of the road.

No need to slow down or lend a hand, I think to myself, and they don't, choosing instead to stare but not get involved.

The important thing is that I want to be seen. If people report a stray running along the road, it will only strengthen the story when I show up at the Horvath home.

A lost dog found. A stray who has come home.

I leave the highway and cut in at Malibu Colony Cove, following a map I memorized at the Maelstrom base. I walk past a guardhouse where two armed security patrolmen are chatting. They notice me at the last second, too late to catch me.

I continue up the road, moving past the doors of multimillion-dollar ocean homes.

I see my destination ahead. It's the house at the very end of the private drive, fronted by a high wall sealing it off from the street around it. It looks exactly like the photos I was shown in my mission briefing.

I walk to the front gate and start to bark—loud staccato bursts that evolve into a mournful howl. It takes only a minute for a hidden door to open. Two bodyguards in black suits step out from the house armed with automatic weapons.

The bodyguards are intimidating as they approach me cautiously. But the moment they get close, their demeanor softens.

"I can't believe it," the first bodyguard says. "Is it Honey?"

Honey! That's the name Magic Myron called me at PetStar.

"It looks just like her," the second one says. "She has the same spots—but I don't recognize this collar."

"Is it you, Honey?"

I'm not sure I like the name, but I bark and wag my tail, playing the part of the dog they know.

"It looks like she's been through a lot."

"You guys have no idea," I say, but of course they only hear barking.

"Poor girl," the first bodyguard says.

The security patrol from the bottom of the street drives up fast. He rolls down the window, acknowledging the guys with automatic weapons from the mansion.

"She came walking up past the guardhouse," the patrolman says. "She's the one, right?"

The bodyguard nods. "It's a miracle."

He opens a door to the mansion property and whistles to me, urging me to follow him.

Inside.

I walk through the door into paradise. A massive ornate house rises before me, fountains and reflecting pools on the grounds in front. The walls of the house are made of glass, and I can look straight through to the length of private beach on the other side. I hear the waves crashing beyond the house and smell the salt foam in the air.

The door of the mansion flies open, and a bright-eyed redheaded girl runs out, her mouth open with awe and delight as she flings herself at me.

It's the girl from my flashbacks.

I look down, and sure enough—she's wearing pink boat shoes.

"Honey, you're home!" she shouts, and she throws her arms around my neck.

The breath catches in my throat as I feel her arms clutching me, and I taste her salty tears as she weeps with joy.

I lean into her, letting her embrace me as Honey, her long-lost pet.

I DO NOT REMEMBER THE HORVATH FAMILY.

Not directly. I have only wisps of memory

that float in and out of my consciousness.

But the family remembers me. I'm their beloved dog, Honey, who disappeared after six months of living with them.

"We don't know how you snuck on board the yacht," Helen Horvath says. "The police found your pawprints on the dock after the yacht sank, and we were so worried about you."

"Joy was heartbroken," Helen's boyfriend says.

Joy. That's the name of the girl who loves me.

For the Horvaths, the last week has been about mourning the loss of their beloved pet and hoping against hope that she had somehow survived.

For me, they've been about fighting for survival while trying to find out who I am.

Now the Horvaths' pet dog has come home again, and it's a time for celebration.

I'm given a bath and examined by a private vet who comes to the house. Ms. Horvath is desperate to know what happened to me and to explain my injuries. Did I run away? Was I in a fight? Was I hit by a car?

The vet sees the wounds healing from my fight in the forest, and he takes them as evidence I've been a stray, perhaps even fought with one of the coyotes that live in the canyons above Malibu. When it's determined that I'm free of rabies or other diseases and safe to be around children, I'm brought back into the center of family life.

After dinner that night, I relax with the family on a roof deck overlooking the ocean. Joy is curled up next to me, snuggling while she plays on her phone.

"Look how happy she is," Ms. Horvath says, smiling at her daughter.

Helen Horvath is one of the richest women in the world. She could afford an unlimited number of dogs, but her daughter bonded with one special dog, a dog who seemed more intelligent than any other, a dog who was unique and irreplaceable.

"I told you everything happens for a reason," her boyfriend says.

I lie on the deck and feel the cool wood planks on my belly. General Rupani said I lived with the Horvath family for six months, but I have no real memory of that. I look around at the family I don't know, and I feel a pang of sorrow, missing Chance and wondering if he's okay.

"Can you hear me, She-Nine?"

I snap up, startled by General Rupani's voice in my

head, broadcasting from a mile away in the command center.

"I hear you."

"You're inside the house?"

"I'm here, and I've been cleared by the vet to interact with the family."

Joy takes the tiara off her head and tries to put it on mine. "Now you're a princess, too," she says.

"It's a little hard to talk right now," I tell the general.

"What are you doing exactly?"

Joy adjusts the tiara, then she dances around me, bowing deeply as if she's meeting royalty.

"I guess I'm bonding," I say.

"Tonight," the general says. "That's when you'll finish your mission."

I WAIT UNTIL THE
FAMILY IS ASLEEP.

I creep through the house, moving down the dark hallway toward Ms. Horvath's room.

"Slow and steady," General Rupani says.

I grunt an acknowledgment and continue down the hall. I pass Joy's bedroom and hear her snoring lightly as she sleeps.

I stop in the middle of the hall, my breath quickening, my pulse speeding up.

"Your heart rate and respiration are too high," General Rupani says. "What's going on with you?"

I hesitate, fighting the instinct to run away before I do something to harm this family.

"You're thinking too much, She-Nine. That's always been your problem. You're too intelligent, and it gets in your way. Follow my commands, and you'll be okay."

"What do you want me to do?" I whisper.

"Helen Horvath's bedroom. Head there now."

I take a deep breath and continue down the hall toward the bedroom, my paws silent on the carpeting.

I glance out the second-floor window of the mansion. A bodyguard walks the property, looking for dangers from outside, unaware that the real danger is me.

I walk toward the bedroom. The door is slightly ajar.

I stop, and a sense of déjà vu washes over me. I've been in this situation before, this same hall, this same moment.

The memory of the blond soldier hits me like a wave. He's wearing a blue Maelstrom uniform, and he's adjusting my collar, just like Rupani did earlier today.

"Keep going," General Rupani says.

I hesitate, struggling as the memory pushes its way into my consciousness.

"You may feel uncertain," the general says, "but you've done this many times before. You're trained and bred for it. Trust your instincts."

I whimper and shake off the memory. I nudge open the bedroom door with my snout. The room is dark, with just a hint of moonlight coming through the drapes. It's more than enough light for me to be able to see everything.

Ms. Horvath is sleeping soundly in a massive bed, her boyfriend next to her. The jump drive glints on a silver chain around her neck.

"Get the drive and take it to the hall window," General Rupani says.

This is the mission I was briefed on earlier, but is it the entire mission?

I take a step toward Helen Horvath, and my body starts

ALLEN ZADOFF

to overheat. My tongue lolls out of the side of my mouth and I hear myself panting.

"What's happening to you?" General Rupani asks.

The scene before me is calm, just a woman and her boyfriend sleeping soundly, yet my body is reacting as if something terrible happened in this room.

I stare at Helen's face in the moonlight, and my memories start to return.

Six months come flooding back to me.

I lived with this family. I gathered evidence on Ms. Horvath implicating her in money-laundering activities overseas. That money was funding terrorism, or so it seemed.

I remember that part now. But there's something else— something more troubling. Not about her, but about me.

About Maelstrom.

Why can't I remember?

"Why didn't I finish the mission before?" I ask General Rupani.

"No matter," he says. "Stop asking questions and get the drive."

Why didn't I finish?

I edge toward the bed, lifting my paws and hoisting myself up as quietly as I can.

Ms. Horvath stirs. "Honey, is that you?" she says, still half-asleep.

I come closer, pushing my weight against her. She reaches for me, instinctively pulling me toward her.

"You're a good dog, Honey. Joy loves you so much."

I snuggle against her and she sighs.

"I'm glad you came home, girl. I don't know what we'd do without you."

The sweetness of her words burns me. I hate myself right now, hate what I'm about to do.

I lick her face and she laughs in her sleep and pushes my head gently away. As she does, I brush past her bare throat, using a tooth to snag the jump drive necklace and pop it from around her neck without her knowing, then catch it in my mouth.

I lean into her, putting too much weight on her leg.

"Get down, Honey," she urges. "Sleep in your own bed. I love you, but I'll see you in the morning."

She pets me and pushes me away at the same time, then she rolls over and goes back to sleep.

"Did you do it?" the general asks.

"Yes," I whisper, barely containing my anger.

I hop off the bed, carrying the jump drive necklace in my mouth. I walk to the hall window and nudge it open with my snout. Then I jump up and drop the necklace outside, watching as a Maelstrom drone whizzes by and snatches it in midair, before rapidly ascending and disappearing over the wall.

There's a pause in the transmission as the general gets confirmation of the pickup. A moment later, his voice is in my head.

"See how easy that was?"

I growl low, anger hot in my chest.

"That's it, then. I'm done. You can let Chance go," I say.

"You're not done yet," the general says.

"What do you mean?"

"You know what I mean," he says ominously.

Just then I remember a different voice, the voice of my former handler.

It's time to finish the job, my handler said.

"What is the real mission?" I ask General Rupani.

"Same as it was before," he says coldly. "Go downstairs and turn on the gas stove."

"What?"

"You'll accidentally turn on the burners as you're trying to get food. This will start the chain of events that will take out Helen Horvath."

I steady myself, the hall spinning around me.

"What about Joy?"

"We left the sprinkler system on in her room."

"She needs her mother."

"You've done it before," General Rupani says. "You're good at making accidents happen."

I whimper and fall back to my hind paws.

"That can't be true." My voice sounds high and strained, almost like it's coming from a different dog.

"These are guilty people, She-Nine. You become their beloved pet, and then you make them disappear. It's your special skill."

"I love people," I say.

"That's where you've gotten confused. Your brain got scrambled by that zapper. You love people so you can hurt them."

"I don't believe you," I whisper.

"If you want to help that boy, you'll go downstairs and finish the job."

The bedroom door down the hall is open, and I can hear Helen Horvath sleeping, her breathing slow and steady. In a room nearby, Joy whispers in her sleep.

"Finish the job," General Rupani says.

I trot downstairs to the kitchen and see the stack of dish towels sitting near the stove. I trace the path from burner, to towels, to drapes, to ceiling.

"You're the family dog," the general says. "You'll panic when you see fire and grab the flaming drape, pulling it down and unintentionally spreading the fire across the room and up the stairs."

"You told me there was a sprinkler system," I say.

"An electrician was working in the home the other day and accidentally cut through the wire that powers the system, everywhere but Joy's room."

"A *Maelstrom* electrician."

"That's right."

I stand in the kitchen, my heart racing as memories of my previous mission flood in.

It was a week ago, and I was in this same home. On the same mission.

In my memory, I'm listening to my former handler, the blond soldier from my nightmares.

"We're adjusting the mission," the handler said. "It's become a termination event."

"Why?" I asked.

"It's not a discussion, it's an order," my handler said.

Now I'm back in the present, standing in the kitchen. And General Rupani is asking me to do the same terrible thing.

"I understand the mission now," I tell the general.

"Good. Then you should have no problem carrying it out."

I think about Chance and the things I'm being asked to do to keep him safe.

I would do anything for him. Anything but this.

That's when a new plan comes to my mind. I turn away from the stove and walk toward the front door.

"The blond soldier," I say. "He was my last handler. He led me on this mission."

I hear a gasp on the line. "Your memory is coming back," General Rupani says.

"Parts of it. What was his name?"

"You never knew his name. You only knew him as your handler."

I think about the younger version of myself I saw on the video in the Maelstrom base. I remember the brown-and-white spotted puppy I used to be training with the blond soldier. I run an obstacle course while my handler looks on. I react to his commands, wanting to please him, carrying out a task, then running toward him, waiting on hind legs to be rewarded with treats. The memory sickens me. I thought these people were teaching me to be a good dog, but they were training me to blindly follow commands so I would kill for them.

"Each dog bonds with a single handler," General Rupani says. "It's part of the training protocol. You're deployed on a mission by your handler, you follow his or her orders, and then you return to the handler."

I walk through the front door and out into the yard.

"Something went wrong a week ago," I say.

"You went wrong. You abandoned the mission and you went rogue, turning on your handler."

In my memory, I refused to hurt the family. I burst out of the house, and I ran to a command trailer down by the beach. I broke in and lunged at my handler, clamping down on his arm, stripping him of the zapper, then attacking him.

His screams are the ones I've been hearing in my nightmares.

I killed him, and then I fled down the beach to the marina and snuck on board the Horvaths' yacht to hide out. I sought the comfort and familiarity of a location I knew, and I judged that Maelstrom wouldn't look for me there, assuming I would run as far as possible from the scene.

But I was wrong. They found me, they zapped me, and then they arranged an accident of their own.

For mc.

"Why are you breathing heavily?" the general asks.

"I'm excited," I say.

I move at lighting speed across the lawn, a blur to the bodyguard, who barely registers my movement. I leap twenty feet in the air, over the wall, and race down Malibu Colony Street.

"You went rogue a week ago," General Rupani says. "We have one rule in Maelstrom: Don't bite the hand that feeds you. When you attacked your handler, you left me no choice. I had to put you down."

"I had good reason to attack him," I say.

"You didn't have any reason. You were clouded by emotion."

"I made a choice to protect the Horvath family," I say.

"We made you intelligent so you would follow orders better, not so you would exercise free will."

The command center is a mile away hidden in the darkness of the beach. The wind carries the scent of metal and electrical components that lead me there.

"This is your second chance," General Rupani says. "Finish the mission and Chance goes free. Then we can discuss bringing you back into Maelstrom."

"All I have to do is follow orders?"

"That's all you ever had to do, She-Nine."

"I have a name," I say. "My name is Wild, and I can think for myself. I know who I am, and what you are. . . ."

I race across the sand, my breath roaring in my ears.

"What am I seeing on the drone footage? Where are you now?" General Rupani shouts.

I ignore him and head for the double trailer of the command center.

Maelstrom soldiers guard the perimeter. I approach them in the dark, but I'm moving too fast for them to defend themselves. I hit them with ferocious kicks, sending them sprawling across the sand.

I smash through the front door of the command center to find twenty or more soldiers looking up, confused. There are complex electronics and monitoring equipment on consoles around them. I see images outside the Horvath house from multiple angles, including a sky view from the drone.

The soldiers realize what's going on and come at me, but I'm moving on instinct, arcing in the air and smashing as I go, a whirlwind of legs and body strikes that take out the entire room in a matter of seconds.

With the first trailer clear, I plow through the inner door into the next.

General Rupani stands on the far side of the trailer. He holds Chance in a vicelike grip, one arm clamped around his shoulders. He holds a zapper in his opposite hand.

It's pressed to Chance's forehead. Chance looks at me, his eyes desperate.

"Let him go," I say, growling deep in my throat.

"I gave you an order in that house," General Rupani says.

"I don't take orders from you."

"I'm your creator," he says through gritted teeth. "You wouldn't exist without me. Maelstrom wouldn't exist."

"Madeline Pao was a creator," I say. "You're just a thief and a murderer."

"Dr. Pao had every opportunity to join us, but she refused."

"She didn't want her technology to be weaponized."

"Weaponized? She barely wanted it to be utilized! She had incredible power at her disposal, and she was wasting it on what? Cute little puppies and babysitter dogs. I was the one with vision. I saw the potential in her technology—the kind of animal we could build. An animal like you. A soldier.

A weapon. You can't deny what you are or what you were born to be."

"I have a choice," I say, baring my teeth at him.

General Rupani laughs and squeezes Chance tighter.

"A choice? You think you chose to be friends with this boy? You're programmed to trick humans into bonding with you. You befriend, you ingratiate, you play the good dog— and then you destroy them. It's what you were created to do, and what you'll always do. You're a killer."

I think about the Maelstrom dog saying that we're alike, and I realize it's not true.

"I killed to save the Horvath family a week ago and to protect Chance yesterday. I don't kill for you. I kill to defend my pack."

"You think Chance is the first kid to love you? What about the Silberstein kids, and the Mercurio brothers before them?"

I'm horrified as I remember Myron saying I'd been to PetStar with different families over the past couple of years. I didn't know what he meant at the time, but now it's becoming clear.

"There have been many families, many kids who think you're their beloved pet," General Rupani says. "You've lied to every one of them. You believe you've been going *against* your instincts this last week with Chance, but you've been following them. You set Chance up to trust you without even knowing it. You made him love you, and you had no idea how much aggression was inside you."

"That's a lie," I say.

"You can't hide from your true nature," the general says. "It's more powerful than you are."

I calculate the distance to Rupani, and I think about his reaction time on the trigger of the weapon.

There's no way I can get to him before he hurts Chance. Which means I'm stuck.

"Turn around and finish the mission," General Rupani says.

There's a sudden movement behind him. From the shadows in the back of the command vehicle, Junebug comes running forward, a zapper in her hands. She raises it toward me, and I step back, thinking she's going to shoot me.

"What are you doing?" General Rupani shouts, his eyes wide.

Junebug abruptly changes direction, swinging the zapper toward her father, using it like a baseball bat and striking the general in the back of the head with a loud *smack*.

General Rupani grunts and his eyes roll back into his head. He immediately lets go of Chance and falls hard, the zapper dropping out of his hand as he collapses on the ground in a heap.

We stand there, shocked, looking at the general's unconscious body.

Chance gasps and runs across the trailer, stopping in front of me. He looks down, his face solemn.

"Tell me it's a lie," he says. "All those terrible things he was saying about you not really being my friend."

I think about our time together this week, all the experiences I've had with Chance and the feelings that have come up as I've gotten to know him.

I bring my face close to his, our noses touching.

"You're my best friend, and I love you," I say. "That's the truth."

"I knew it!" he shouts, and he flings his arms around me, squeezing so tight that it hurts. I lick his face and yelp as he grabs my fur, hanging on for dear life, the two of us laughing and rolling on the floor together.

"Hey, how about a little credit up here?"

We both look up to see Junebug standing over us.

"I'm the one who knocked him out, right?"

"You were amazing!" Chance says. "Where have you been all this time?!"

Before I can stop him, he grabs her, pulling her down to the floor with us.

"You saved both of us," he says.

She shrugs. "You guys are cool. And my dad can be a real jerk sometimes."

Chance sits up fast and his face goes pale. "What did you just say?"

"My dad sucks."

Chance looks from Junebug to me, confused.

"The general is her father," I tell him.

"Your dad runs Maelstrom? So you knew what was happening all along?"

"Kind of. Yeah."

"But . . . but you were trying to save us," Chance stammers.

She sighs. "I guess Wild isn't the only one who went rogue."

"This whole thing is tripping me out," Chance says.

I look at her, trying to understand a girl who defies her father, yet seems to have allegiance to him, too.

"I have some explaining to do," Junebug says. "It started when—"

A door slams loudly, and we all jump up, startled.

"The general's gone!" Chance shouts.

"Where did he go?" I ask.

"There's a secret door!" Junebug points.

In the back of the trailer, I see a hidden trapdoor, its hinges buried in the floor.

"He's going to get away," Junebug shouts.

"No, he's not," I promise.

I DIVE THROUGH THE TRAPDOOR AND DROP ONTO THE BEACH.

I stand in the sand and sniff in every direction, trying to pinpoint General Rupani before he can get too far. I lock on to him and hear the sound at the same time—an engine roaring to life down the beach.

I race out from under the command center and look downwind. There, in the light of the moon, I see the general sitting in a beach buggy. He revs the engine and takes off, thick tires kicking up sand.

"RUPANI!" I shout, but he's turned off the comms gear so I can't communicate with him.

I won't let him get away.

I sprint after the buggy, my paws struggling to gain traction in the loose sand. His buggy is built for this terrain, but it can only go so fast, and I start to gain on him. He glances nervously over his shoulder and sees me behind him, so he pushes the engine hard, accelerating from ten miles per hour to twenty, to thirty.

That only makes me angrier, and I give it everything I've got, ignoring the burning pain in my legs as I chase him. The buggy is moving so fast, it hits a sand dune and goes airborne. For a moment I think he's going to wipe out, but he's an even better driver than Junebug, and he hits the sand and regains control, turning the wheel hard to keep from tipping over before accelerating again.

I've gained on him in the last few seconds, moving within striking distance.

I think I can make it.

I'm preparing to leap the last few feet when he surprises me by cutting the wheel toward the ocean and driving directly into the waves.

The engine roars as it hits water, and I watch with amazement as the buggy converts into an amphibious vehicle that can float.

He looks back at me standing on the beach, and I see a smile cross his face. He thinks he's gotten away from me.

"Not so fast, Rupani."

I run and jump high into the air, and I can see his eyes widen in surprise as I splash into the water. I immediately start to swim, the cold water shocking my skin. I'm determined to get to this man on land or sea.

I poke my head above the waves and start to doggy-paddle, racing after him as fast as I can. It seems like I might have a chance, but then a propeller whirs to life on the back of the buggy. It churns up foam, and within seconds the buggy gains speed and motors out to sea, moving faster than I could ever swim.

I have no choice but to tread water as I watch it disappear. General Rupani is gone.

The emotions of the day catch up to me, and I look up at the moon, exhausted. I breathe in the moist air, letting the water cool my overheated body.

The waves lap at my fur, and I taste salt water on my lips. I laugh as I realize I'm in the Pacific Ocean, only a few miles from where the yacht sank, where all of this began.

It was only a few days ago, but it seems like a lifetime.

I spent days searching for my home, and then I found it. Maelstrom was my home. But not anymore.

I turn and swim back toward the shore.

THE SUN IS RISING
OVER MALIBU BEACH.

I paddle toward the shore and smell something burning. I see smoke carried on the breeze from the direction of the command center. I swim faster and haul myself onto the beach, shaking vigorously as I race toward the source of the smoke.

The command center is ablaze, flames dancing in the wind.

Junebug and Chance stand fifty feet away, watching it burn.

"What happened here?" I ask.

"I think one of the weapons went off and accidentally ignited the trailer," Chance says.

"Definitely accidental," Junebug says. "Maelstrom makes accidents happen, and now they're the victims of an accident."

She grins defiantly and trades conspiratorial glances with Chance.

"Where are the rest of the soldiers?" I ask.

"They ran away once the general was gone," Chance says with a laugh. "The ones who could still run. The ones you fought against had to be carried away by their friends."

Chance and Junebug are relaxed and smiling, delighted by Maelstrom's retreat. I look at the burning command center, the smoke wafting into the air, and I do not feel the same sense of relief. We may have won the battle, but I fear the war is far from over.

I turn to Junebug, and I can see the orange flames reflected in her eyes.

"I'm confused about something," I say. "Were you lying to us the whole time?"

"Not lying," she says. "I really did steal my father's car and drive to PetStar to get you guys."

"But why?" Chance asks.

"I was monitoring his soldiers on my comms equipment. When I saw they were after you and Wild, I wanted to help you. At first just to get back at him. Later it was for other reasons."

"What kinds of reasons?" Chance asks curiously.

"I got to know you both," she says, her cheeks turning red. "Then I started to like you. It's pretty cool to have friends."

The wind shifts, and smoke wafts toward us. Junebug blinks tears from her eyes. She squints and looks down at me.

"I'm sorry I lied about who I was, Wild. And also

how much I knew about you. Do you guys think you can forgive me?"

She's always been so confident, but now I see the vulnerability in her eyes.

Chance looks at me, uncertain how to respond.

I think of Junebug slamming her father in the back of the head and saving Chance in the process. Whatever happened earlier on the mountain, knocking out her father was proof enough of her loyalty.

"I can forgive you," I say.

"What about you, Chance?" she asks, nervously twirling the blue stripe in her hair.

"You were really trying to save us from Maelstrom?" he asks.

"Why else would I risk my life all those times for you? I got scared when Wild killed that dog, and I called the soldiers. It was a dumb thing to do. I see that now."

Chance stares at her for a long minute.

"I've done dumb things before," he says. "I guess I forgive you."

Junebug smiles, relieved.

There's a loud crash as the roof of the command center collapses.

"The Horvaths will be waking up soon. They'll call the police when they see the smoke."

"We should get moving," Junebug says. "Oh, and before we go"—she reaches into her pocket and pulls out a silver cell phone—"I fixed your phone, Chance."

Chance grabs the phone and presses the power button. A moment later the screen glows blue.

"How did you—" The screen chimes, and Chance stares at the phone. "My mom texted! She said she'd see me later."

Junebug smiles. "Not bad, right?"

Chance looks at her in awe as we walk together to the parking lot at the edge of the beach.

"So you're going to meet your mom now?" Junebug asks.

Chance glances at me for confirmation, and I wag my tail.

"We're all going together," Chance says.

"I can't come with you," Junebug says.

"What do you mean? I'll tell my mom you need a place to stay. You can live with us."

"You know that won't work."

"You can't go home after what happened with your father," I tell her.

"I'm not going home. I'll stay with my aunt. She's the only one my father's scared of. He wouldn't dare do anything with her around."

"Are you sure?" Chance says, biting his lip anxiously.

She comes closer, her hair blowing in the wind.

"I'll be fine. Besides, it's my family," she says. "It might be messed up, but it's the only one I have."

"I hear that," Chase replies.

Junebug suddenly kneels down in front of me. I think she's going to hug me good-bye, but instead she pulls me close and whispers in my ear.

"Your collar does more than you think it does. Keep exploring."

There's a small explosion as a propane tank in one of the trailers ignites, and I hear sirens in the distance.

"I gotta cruise," she says. "I don't want to be around when the cops get here, and neither do you."

She throws us a wave, then runs down the beach and disappears through the smoke.

"What did she say to you?" Chance asks.

"Nothing important," I say, but I'm already thinking about my collar and wondering what Junebug meant.

The police sirens are coming closer, and I tug at Chance's pant leg, urging him away.

Together we walk up the road to a bus stop where we can grab the Metro back to Santa Monica.

WE'RE STANDING OUTSIDE A DRUG TREATMENT FACILITY IN CULVER CITY.

Chance stands on the sidewalk next to me, tapping his foot anxiously as he waits for his mother to appear.

"It's going to be okay," I say, but I feel the same anticipation.

A minute later the facility door opens, and a woman steps out. She's about thirty-five years old, pretty, wearing tight jeans and a loose white T-shirt, and carrying a backpack over one shoulder. She has messy brown hair, the same color as Chance's. She looks around uncertainly, biting her lower lip.

"Mom!" Chance shouts.

Surprise turns to delight on the woman's face as she sees Chance and me waiting for her.

"Chancey!" she shouts, and she rushes forward, throwing her arms out wide.

Chance races across the street and leaps into her arms, and I'm flooded with a sense of relief.

Chance's mom squeezes him tight, the two of them laughing and crying at the same time. He hops down and she holds his face in her hands, staring at him, running her fingers through his hair and across his face, like she's memorizing every detail.

"Mom, I want you to meet someone."

He grabs her hand and pulls her across the street toward me.

"Someone? You mean the dog?"

"Her name is Wild," he says.

"Wild? That's a scary name, isn't it? Whose dog is this?"

"She's her own dog, Mom. And she's not scary. She's my friend."

Chance's mom nods, looking me over. After a moment she smiles.

"Nice to meet you, Wild," she says, and she reaches out and immediately pets my head like someone who's never had a dog before. She should relax and hold her hand out for me to sniff, giving us a little time to get acquainted. She does it all wrong, but it doesn't bother me. She's Chance's mother, and I want to meet her.

She steps back and examines me, hands on her hips.

"I wouldn't call her cute exactly," she says. "More like athletic. But there's something unusual about her. She has intelligent eyes."

"She's really smart," Chance says, throwing me a wink. He puts his hand on my back, gently stroking my fur. I feel a wave of pleasure flow down my spine.

Chance's mom sighs, looking at me. "How on earth did

you get a dog at the group home? I thought they were pretty strict."

"You gotta know how to work the system," Chance says with a grin.

"Speaking of the system, we have to get to court," his mom says, "but I want to hear all about it later."

"We're ready to go," Chance says, and he pats my head again.

"We? Yeah, um, about the dog—"

"We have to take her," he says. "I can't go without her."

A cab pulls up in front of the center and beeps.

"That's our ride," Chance's mom says.

"What about Wild?"

His mom bites her lower lip, just like I've seen Chance do.

"Okay, we'll figure it out," she says. "You, me, and Wild."

Chance pumps his fist in celebration.

"I need to talk to you alone," I tell him.

"I'll catch up to you in a second, Mom."

She crosses the street, and Chance turns his back and kneels down, blocking his mother's view so she won't see us talking.

"Isn't Mom great?" he says.

I nuzzle his hand with my nose. "I'm not coming with you," I say.

Chance looks startled. He stares at me, his mouth open.

"What are you talking about? Mom said it was okay. We can be a family now."

"The general won't give up. As long as I'm in the world, his secret is out."

"We'll go where they can't find us."

The cab honks, and Chance's mother calls to him from the open window.

"If I stay with you, you'll never be safe," I say.

Chance starts weeping, his body heaving against mine as he holds me in his arms.

I lick his face, taste the salt of his tears on my tongue.

"Where will you go?" he asks.

"I'll find someplace."

"But you'll be all alone!"

"I want you and your mom to have a life together," I say. "She needs you. You need each other."

"I don't want to say good-bye."

"Maybe we can say something else." I nuzzle his hand again, breathing in his scent.

"Like what?"

"How about, *Just for now*?" I look into his eyes. A dog and her boy. A boy and his dog.

Chance wipes his eyes and smiles thinly. "Not good-bye. *Just for now*."

His mother calls to him. "Chance! We have to leave now or we're going to be late."

He stands up, his eyes locked on mine.

"The earbud," I say softly.

"But if I give it up, we can't—"

"I'll hold on to it for you," I say. "Until the next time."

"Promise?"

He reluctantly takes the earbud from his ear. He presses the button on my collar, and I hear the mechanical swish of the collar box opening. He replaces the earbud and the box closes again.

"You're my friend forever," I say.

Chance points to his ear. "I only hear barking now."

I whimper and shuffle in place, trying not to cry out and upset him even more.

Chance looks at me for a long moment, then he jogs across the street to join his mom.

I watch him the whole way, waiting until he's safely in the back of the cab.

"I thought you were bringing the dog?" I hear his mother saying.

"She can't come," Chance says.

Those are the last words I hear as I turn and trot away down the street, my heart begging me to stay, but my head knowing that I'm doing what must be done.

I RUN THROUGH
A DOG PARK.

The park is located in a large and beautiful
recreation area filled with baseball diamonds and soccer
fields. I race from one side of the fenced park to the other,
watching as dog packs form and separate around me, the
dogs leaping and barking as they play.

I don't engage with any pack, choosing instead to stay on
the side, low-key, not revealing myself in any way.

A big friendly retriever brings a length of rope in his
teeth, trying to get me to grab it and play tug-of-war
with him.

I sniff at the rope, then I take it in my teeth. I taste
the saliva of the many dogs who have fought over this toy
earlier in the day. I shake my head back and forth, enjoying the sound of the rope whistling in the wind. After a few
shakes I get bored and drop it on the ground.

"Not really my thing," I say.

The retriever is confused. He grabs the rope and runs off
to find a dog he can play with.

A woman appears in front of me, looking to my collar for a name.

"Who do you belong to?" she says in a singsong voice like she's talking to a child.

I ignore her, turn away, and break into a trot, speeding up as I move through the dog park, passing animals playing and play-fighting, some on leashes and some off, but all of them with owners waiting.

I run toward the fence that encloses the dog park, gaining speed as I go. I leap high, easily clearing the top of the fence.

"One got out!" a man shouts, trying to find my owner.

He shouts for me to stop, but I don't listen. I race across the park, through the baseball field and farther still, leaving the dogs behind as I sprint into the tree line.

I continue until I no longer hear humans or dogs, until the only sound is the slap of my paws against the ground, the breath in my lungs, and my heart pounding in my chest as I run free.

ACKNOWLEDGMENTS

This book marks the beginning of many new relationships for me, and I'd like to say thanks:

To Sarah Davies and the wonderful folks at Greenhouse Lit for inviting me to join the family.

To Kieran Viola, who championed the book and gave it a home.

To Mary Pender for her enthusiasm and vision.

Finally, a very special thanks to my old friends Barry Lyga and Paul Griffin for reminding me to keep the faith . . . one word at a time.